YOUNGER GALT
Laura lives herself

Younger Galt

Laura lives herself

A Story

Title of the original edition,
published by BoD – Books on Demand, Norderstedt:
"Laura lebt selbst"
"Erzählung"
© 2020 Galt, Younger

Second revised edition
© 2021 Galt, Younger

Bibliographic Information of the German National Library:
The German National Library lists this publication in the
German National Bibliography; detailed bibliographic data are
available on the Internet at http://dnb.dnb.de.

First english edition
© 2021 Galt, Younger

Production and publishing: BoD – Books on Demand,
Norderstedt

ISBN: 9783753407593

Contents

This story and the characters, companies and products portrayed are fictitious and without real role models (with the exception of the Nobel Prize winners mentioned by name).

However, the situations described are real.
They occur thousands of times a day.

Admissions Office

Laura looked at the official in astonishment.

"What skills do I lack to produce this blood pressure monitor?

I developed it by myself and built a prototype. An independent body has confirmed that it meets the accuracy of a medical device; although I don't want to use it for medical purposes at all."

"Your blood pressure monitor is a medical device. To manufacture it, you need specific training and a company that has an officially approved workflow."

"I wrote in my application that I will not offer the blood pressure monitor for medical purposes and that I don't want to obtain a licence for my company to build medical devices."

"It is a device for measuring blood pressure and therefore it is a medical device."

"That is not in any of the legal texts."

"But that is in accordance with the law."

"Where can I look that up?"

"I say this.

If you don't like it, you can contact the complaints department of the Admissions Office. If you have any further questions, contact the helpdesk on the first floor. Good afternoon."

Order

The official was staring grimly at his screen. He thought the brat was only twenty-one years old, according to the documents presented, and now she believes she will become a great entrepreneur. She even thought she could argue with him.

The idea that a twenty-one-year-old woman could set up a business was deeply abhorrent to him.

She should drudge for ten years as an employee in an office, he thought, just as he did every day, instead of collecting big money without much work.

How did the brat ever come to believe that at twenty-one she could shape her professional life according to her own will? He would not allow this social injustice.

He thought that in his office people have to play by his rules.

His leverage was the possibility of the medical application of the device. He had quickly recognised this and was pleased.

If she had been willing to pay, he thought, he would have been willing to negotiate, but considering her age she probably didn't have enough money for it.

He spat in the flowerpot and remembered that he must be careful not to be five minutes late for lunch again today.

Laura

Laura was walking to her car and thinking about what had happened.

Based on her previous experience as an entrepreneur, she had not expected that cooperation with the Admissions Office would be easy. However, she had not expected a total blockade.

Laura had completed her general education three years ago and immediately afterwards had become self-employed as a computer consultant for smaller companies. She had acquired the knowledge for this herself during her school years. At that time, she had already started to support individual entrepreneurs with minor software problems.

She had come to the idea of building a blood pressure monitor through her grandmother, who owned one. The device had broken down. Her grandmother had bought a new one and given Laura the old one. Laura had disassembled it and figured out how it worked. Little by little, over the last five years, she had been thinking about improvements.

To supplement her knowledge, she had attended a three-year distance learning course at a mechatronics technical school, which she had just completed two weeks ago.

Now that formal proof of her expertise had been provided, she wanted to set up a company to build her improved blood pressure monitors.

She had saved the necessary start-up capital from the money she had earned as a computer consultant.

Well, she thought, this bureaucracy is worse than I imagined, but the hurdles will not be insurmountable.

She decided to contact the Employers' Association. During her previous entrepreneurial activities, she had not identified any useful assistance from the Employers' Association and had therefore not thought about membership.

While she was thinking about further steps, she swerved to the right and strolled across the zebra crossing.

A van braked abruptly in front of the zebra crossing. She looked up and saw that it was a plumber's van with two workers in it.

She looked at them and raised her hand half apologetically, half gratefully.

Once she was on the other side of the road, one of the workers lowered the window and called out after her: "You've lost something!"

Laura looked back and saw nothing. She looked at the worker questioningly.

"Your pace," he said and winked at her.

Laura had to laugh. The two workers drove on grinning.

No, she thought to herself, I don't lose that so easily.

Employers' Association

"The Employers' Association can definitely help you," said the head of the Employers' Association in a determined voice.

Laura was sitting on a comfortable sofa in his spacious office. He had settled on the other wing of the sofa. In front of them, coffee and biscuits were set out on a low glass table.

The head of the Employers' Association was not an entrepreneur himself, but a manager in an international corporation. Among other things, his company manufactured medical products, including blood pressure monitors for medical applications.

Laura had told him of her problem.

The fact that Laura had come into direct contact with the head of the Employers' Association was thanks to its public relations department. This department had developed a policy whereby he should personally deal with a request every few months. This was to signal that the Employers' Association was an institution with a flat hierarchy, where everyone felt responsible for the problems of the entrepreneurs.

As Laura's enquiry concerned blood pressure monitors and did not appear to be very complex, the assistant from the public relations department had suggested that the enquiry be handled by the head of the Employers' Association.

The head of the Employers' Association sipped his coffee and turned his head towards the window with his chin raised.

He looked out thoughtfully.

Then he turned his head towards Laura with his chin raised and looked at her.

"I advise you," he said in a thoughtful voice, "to buy this brand of coffee. It tastes excellent."

He continued dynamically, "The Employers' Association is an important link between entrepreneurs, politics and administration. It is important that there is such a consensual and interdisciplinary level of discussion for the integral solution of comprehensive problems.

I had dinner only a fortnight ago with the Minister for Economic Affairs and a senior ministerial official."

He remained silent for a moment to let the meaning of the statement sink in.

His secretary came in. "Your barber on line three," she breathed busily.

"You'll excuse me," he said decisively to Laura.

Laura got up and left.

Curiosity and Joy

It was shortly after midnight, and Laura was sitting in her office. On the screen in front of her she was viewing a drawing of the latest version of the circuit board with the electronic components for her blood pressure monitor.

She had started designing the circuit board five years ago. At that time, she knew little about electronics, as she was mainly interested in computer operating systems and software development.

Her first prototype had been a simple plug-in board into which the electronic components could be plugged without soldering. The central component was already a programmable microcontroller that served to process the recorded data in order to provide the user with a diverse range of information and to control the blood pressure monitor by means of software.

She remembered what a joy and triumph it had been for her to complete the first prototype with all its functions.

Since that first prototype, the circuit board had gone through many stages of development. As her knowledge and skills had increased, the circuit board had improved from one version to the next. Time and again she had experienced the joy and satisfaction of holding an improved version of the circuit board in her hands.

She had started to solder the components onto the circuit board that she had etched herself. Later, when the circuit board was becoming increasingly optimised and the components more compact, she had outsourced its production to external manufacturers, as it was no longer possible to do it manually.

She had started to simulate the behaviour of the circuit board and the components on the computer in order to make further improvements.

Now, in front of her on the screen was the final version of her efforts, intended for the blood pressure monitors that were scheduled for sale.

Euphorically, Laura looked at the result she saw before her and thought with impatient enthusiasm that she could improve it even more in the years to come.

Satisfied and proud, she leaned back in her chair and crossed her hands behind her head.

"I have the most beautiful job in the world," she said aloud and looked at the screen laughing.

Taio

Laura was in the showroom of a company that sold 3D printers for the production of plastic parts. Laura's blood pressure monitor had a plastic casing and a number of other small plastic parts.

The owner of the company, a young man a few years older than Laura, was sitting opposite her behind his desk.

He had spent the last few hours enthusiastically presenting Laura with suitable printers for her job.

Laura had had the functionality and capabilities of the various printers explained to her. She was fascinated by the possibilities that these devices offered for her production.

In their excitement, the two of them had got involved in a deep technical discussion. They then realised with astonishment that three hours had passed.

"When do you plan to start?" asked the young man.

"That's not quite certain yet," said Laura. She told him about her experience at the Admissions Office and with the head of the Employers' Association.

"Satisfying the state institutions is one of the most difficult tasks to be accomplished as an entrepreneur in our state," replied the young man.

"In these cases, I often work with a lawyer who has given me very good advice in the past. I can only recommend her to you. Would you like to have her contact details?"

"Gladly," said Laura.

He wrote them down for her.

The young man told her about problems the lawyer had helped him with. Then they talked some more about his company's foundation and Laura's previous entrepreneurial activities as a computer consultant.

They shook hands as they said goodbye.

"I wish you every success with your business, Laura." He faltered, blushed and started looking for Laura's business card in his files. "I mean, Ms ..."

Laura laughed. "Laura's okay."

"Taio," he replied, and they shook hands laughing once more.

As Laura stepped into the sunlight of the street, she caught herself smiling at the thought that working with this company was a good decision, not only from a technical point of view.

Support

"You're right," said the lawyer.

"That's not stated in the law and is only a personal opinion of the responsible official. In theory, one can certainly object to it."

The lawyer and Laura were sitting opposite each other at a desk in the lawyer's office.

"What do you mean by 'in theory'?" asked Laura.

"Well, you've got to set in motion a sluggish apparatus if you want to take legal action. That costs a lot of time and money. You may not want to take that much time, and you may not have that much money."

"I was told you're a specialist in such admission procedures. I thought this kind of thing often happened."

The lawyer sighed and looked at Laura.

"Look, things are different. The officials at the Admissions Office shy away from such issues. On the one hand, it's exhausting for them. They have to argue objectively and give an account to their superiors about why they're causing trouble. On the other hand, this all happens during their working hours, and their procedural costs are paid for by the state. This means they get angry, and then they block it and take their time.

To put it plainly, I could convince those responsible directly and show my gratitude for their cooperation. This is the fastest and most productive way."

Laura shook her head angrily.

"I don't believe in corruption. I don't want to break any laws. I don't want to have to bribe civil servants to do their normal jobs and let me do mine."

The lawyer sighed again. "I'm also deeply repulsed by corruption, but take a realistic look at the situation.

Firstly, you're not breaking any laws, as we've just discussed. You're simply exposed to the arbitrariness of an official who interprets laws according to his views. Or rather, interprets them according to his intentions.

Secondly, an official appeal over the whole procedure would cost you at least five times the amount of the bribe but with a completely unpredictable outcome. The staff of the appellate body are also civil servants, who usually stand by their colleagues."

"How much is this?"

"Four thousand; for one thousand you get an invoice, that's my fee."

Laura frowned. This would be her income for two months, provided she could bring in enough orders.

She nodded to the lawyer. "Alright, let's do the four thousand."

Trade Regulation

"State regulation of entrepreneurship is obviously a very undefined and arbitrary thing," Laura remarked.

The lawyer shrugged her shoulders. "A historical mixture. Various groups of craftsmen have probably always tried to keep out the competition by forming groups like guilds or the like. At the same time, rulers granted licences for various special activities because it was an easy way to make money and gain favour with them.

The bureaucratic apparatus of the state, which continued to develop, then found in these restrictions a welcome justification for their own existence and a welcome additional source of income, as your case again shows."

"However, the reasoning that this can achieve better quality for the customers seems to be very specious," said Laura.

"Keeping out competition and justifying one's own bureaucratic existence are not very noble goals at first sight," replied the lawyer, "even though they're certainly desirable for the beneficiaries.

No one will openly state these objectives. Of course, more noble goals such as quality, safety or reliability are stated.

However, in practice, it has been shown time and again that only competition and choice for the customer can promote these goals. If the customer isn't satisfied, then he won't buy any more, and word gets around when a manufacturer delivers defective goods. The market is the best guarantee for quality."

"There is no doubt about it," said Laura. "If my product is poor, my company will fail. The customers will decide that."

Interdependent Representatives

"I had a consultation with the Employers' Association about the matter, but it didn't really help at all."

Laura told the lawyer about her conversation with the head of the Employers' Association.

"Oh well, you've come to the right man, I've already had the opportunity to meet that gentleman," replied the lawyer.

"But don't worry about it. If you'd gone to an advice centre of the Employers' Association, things wouldn't have been as strange as in your case, but in the end, you wouldn't have received any more help.

Our Employers' Association is far too interwoven with politics. The people who are in charge there are more interested in their own advantages regarding government contracts and government support programmes. Entrepreneurs who simply want to offer their products on the free market without entering into strange friendship arrangements with the civil service or politicians don't join this association at all."

Laura looked at her in astonishment.

"You should be glad that membership of our Employers' Association is voluntary. There are countries where membership of a quasi-state Employers' Association is compulsory.

There, the Employers' Association and politics are even more interwoven, and the officials of the Employers' Association are at the same time representatives of political parties.

This results in a completely opaque web of interests, and as a compulsory member you have to finance the whole thing without having any benefits from it.

Only recently I heard that the head of such an Employers' Association used up more money from compulsory membership fees in a single ball night than an average compulsory member has money to live on for a whole year."

Flora

"You have been expelled from school?"

Laura looked at her sister Flora in amazement.

Flora was four years younger than Laura. Until recently, she had attended the graduating class of the school Laura had graduated from.

The two of them were sitting in Laura's flat during dinner.

"For what reason?"

"Because I allegedly set a bad example to my classmates by encouraging them to act independently," replied Flora.

Flora did not seem very depressed. Laura knew that Flora had a very open-minded and cheerful nature. She could not remember ever having seen her angry or depressed.

"Tell me what happened."

"I gave some of my classmates tutoring in mathematics, and they got better grades as a result."

"Well, that's no reason to expel you."

"As a result, my classmates often missed mathematics lessons because the teacher's lessons were poor, and they didn't expect to learn anything more from him."

"Are you now blamed for that?"

"I've missed class a few times," continued Flora. "After all, it is not a compulsory school, and I was able to acquire knowledge faster and better on my own.

I see no point in wasting my time in a class that's of no use to me, because I already know everything that's presented anyway.

No teacher seemed bothered that I was absent. On top of that, I have always had very good grades.

At first, the absence of the other pupils was also ignored. The whole thing only kicked off when some pupils cancelled their other private mathematics tuition."

Laura looked surprised.

"It's like this," explained Flora, "the tutoring was given by our mathematics teacher, and he must have lost a considerable amount of money due to the cancellation of his private lessons. He then told us that our behaviour was contrary to the school rules and that he would report this to the headmaster."

Laura nodded. "You were all expelled from school as a result?"

"No," continued Flora, "the headmaster then announced that in future, unexcused absences would immediately lead to expulsion from school because they contradict the State Regulations for Secondary Schools. At the same time, he issued an amnesty for all absences to date.

But the amnesty doesn't apply to me because I was said to have caused the absences of others by my bad example."

"But the other pupils stayed away because the teacher's lessons didn't bring any added value," said Laura. "Didn't you bring that up?"

Flora shrugged. "I don't want to waste my time with such petty discussions."

"Will you repeat the final year at another school?"

"No, I'll take the exams at a private school, although I don't think I'll need the qualifications any time soon. I think it's a waste of time to put myself in a class especially for this."

"But that costs something," said Laura.

"Yes, but thanks to the tutoring I've earned enough money. In addition, I now have enough time for other projects that I've been planning for a long time."

Laura smiled at her.

"Your positive attitude is always a joyful experience for me, little sister."

Flora laughed. "Thanks, big sister."

Independent Action

"It is a special concern of mine that we educate our students to be independently thinking people."

The headmaster looked at the teachers sitting in front of him.

The teachers nodded in agreement.

"They should be able to shape their lives on the basis of their own reason and be able to defend themselves intellectually against external constraints."

The teachers nodded in agreement.

"The education of young people to become independently thinking and acting citizens is the main task of every teacher."

The teachers nodded in agreement.

"Now, the case of Flora." The headmaster looked at his papers.

"In a conversation with me, she admitted, based on a rational assessment, she had come to the conclusion that it was most reasonable for her only to attend the exams at school, as the lessons did not provide her with any additional knowledge.

According to her rational assessment, it was more efficient for her to acquire the knowledge herself.

In addition, she also gave private lessons in mathematics to other pupils. These pupils then stayed away from class because, according to their statements, they could no longer learn anything new there.

Flora has thus disregarded the school rules and incited others to do the same."

The teachers nodded in agreement.

"Students must submit to the school rules and not act independently on the basis of their own considerations."

The teachers nodded in agreement.

"The education of young people to become obedient citizens is the main task of every teacher."

The teachers nodded in agreement.

"Students should live their lives according to the rules of state institutions and not follow their own reason."

The teachers nodded in agreement.

"It is of particular concern to me that we educate our students to be people who absolutely adhere to the rules set by state institutions."

The teachers nodded in agreement.

"I have made arrangements for Flora to leave our school."

The teachers nodded in agreement.

Social Injustice

The official stared at the file in a disgruntled way.

This must have been the brat, he thought to himself, who was here in the office some time ago. Now it seemed that she had managed to get permission to set up a production company for her blood pressure monitor.

He slapped his hand on the table. He had to cough and spit in the flowerpot.

He didn't really care about Laura personally. Five minutes after their conversation in his office he had already forgotten her. He had no fundamental interest in his work and hardly cared about it at all.

What really annoyed him was that someone else had now cashed in. He had misjudged her. He had thought that, as she had no income yet, she would not be able to pay. Moreover, she had seemed too bitchy for him to be someone who would have been willing to pay.

He cursed to himself. Next time he would be more aggressive and make sure that he got his share of the bribe. It was only socially just that he got his share of the entrepreneurs' profits. He cursed about the social injustice in life.

Angrily, he pushed the file aside and stared out the window.

Creativity and Joy

"This is fascinating," exclaimed Laura.

Laura and Taio were standing at the edge of a factory workshop that Laura had rented for her new company.

In front of them stood a table with a computer and a 3D printer. Laura had leased the printer from Taio. He had put it into operation and given Laura a briefing.

Laura had previously created a 3D model of the blood pressure monitor's casing on the computer using a CAD program.

In the course of the briefing, they had imported the 3D model into the printer's control program. Taio had given her some ideas on how the shape of the casing could be optimised for 3D printing.

So, they had got into a discussion and further optimised the draft. Before they knew it, several hours had passed.

Then they had sent the result to the printer and the finished case was now in front of them.

"Yes," said Taio, "I'm always fascinated by it too, although I work with it every day."

"I'd like to continue working on the design all night long and make improvements," said Laura. "I love my work."

"I find it impressive what you put up here," said Taio.

They looked with satisfaction at the result of their work in front of them and found themselves yawning at the same time.

They laughed at each other, and then they fell silent.

They were looking into each other's eyes and slowly leaning towards each other and Laura's phone rang shrilly.

Both startled. Laura looked at the display of her phone.

"A supplier." She took the call.

When she had finished, Taio asked, "Do you want to go out for dinner? My treat."

"Gladly," replied Laura and smiled at him.

Prison

Laura choked in shock and had a coughing fit. Flora patted her on the back with her flat hand.

The two of them were sitting in Laura's flat during dinner.

"You're going to prison?" asked Laura incredulously. "Why?"

"You remember the three big apple trees that Grandma's neighbours own?"

"Yes. Did you cut them down?" asked Laura, trying to make a forced joke.

"Oh no, I picked the apples with the permission of the neighbours. They'd no use for them."

"And?" asked Laura.

"It was over a hundred kilos. I sold them by the road in small quantities."

"And?" asked Laura again.

"Someone reported me to the tax authorities."

"Surely you don't have to pay tax for such a small amount of money, or have those projects you were talking about already started that you could have earned so much?"

"No, but I should have reported it to the tax authorities."

"You don't have to go to prison for that."

"Indirectly. I got a penalty notice and could choose to pay a fifty or to go to prison for three days. As I thought it more convenient, I chose prison."

"For a fifty? You could have got it from me."

"I know, but it wasn't that," said Flora happily. "I wanted to think about a new project in peace anyway. That suits well."

Laura wanted to point out to her that prison was not as carefree as Flora apparently imagined. But she refrained from doing so because she knew that Flora with her carefree curiosity would not understand it.

"Don't look so concerned," said Flora. "If I paid the money, it wouldn't make any difference to prison.

During the time I'd work to earn the fine, I'd be just a prisoner of the state."

Laura sighed. "I'm afraid you're right."

Protection Money

Laura, her tax consultant and two tax officials were sitting in her office, which was located on the edge of her rented factory workshop.

In the hours before, the two officials had carried out a tax audit, which had mainly concerned Laura's previous work as a self-employed computer consultant.

They now held a final meeting.

"Your job as a computer consultant is very lucrative. The back tax payment will amount to a thousand. You will receive a notice," said one of the tax officials.

Laura looked at the two tax officials in amazement.

"You have not found any irregularities or errors. Why do I have to pay back taxes?"

"Well, if you'd prefer, we could continue to examine."

"I'd love you to, but you won't find anything. It's all correct."

"I've no doubt that we'll find nothing," replied the tax official. "But it'll cost you more if we continue to investigate.

If we carry on checking for two more days, the tax consultant alone, who must be present, will cost you a thousand. You'll get off cheaper if you make a lump sum payment."

"Is that legal?" asked Laura astonished.

"If you insult me, I'll file charges against you," replied the tax official.

"Nobody wants to offend you," replied Laura's tax consultant. "Excuse us for a moment."

He gently pulled Laura by the sleeve from the office into the workshop. They walked to the opposite side of the workshop.

"I can only recommend that you respond to the tax officer's request, even if I personally would earn more if the audit were to be continued," the tax consultant explained.

"But I'm supposed to pay arrears, even though I've taxed everything correctly, and the reason given is that otherwise I'll suffer a loss that would be greater than the arrears. This is extortion. It's protection money. It can't be legal."

"Well, officially it is simply declared as another examination, so there is nothing illegal about it," replied the tax consultant. "Of course, it clearly has the character of a protection racket. You have to pay so that no harm is done to you.

The problem isn't only the days of further examination. The auditors can come back at any time they want. You can be sure that they'll do so if they're upset. This will cost you a lot, the payments to me, your time and the time of your employees, during which you will not be able to work productively and earn money."

"Why do the officials carry out such a nasty business?" asked Laura. "I don't understand. What do they get out of it?"

"Well, many people benefit from your money," explained the tax consultant.

"The examiners themselves are rewarded for successful work, even if this isn't officially fixed at the amount brought in, as are their superiors.

Then, of course, it is also a justification of the civil service apparatus. You've probably read in the newspapers several times that the union of tax officials and many politicians are calling for more auditors to be hired. Because, they say, their auditing activities bring the state more money than they cost.

However, since not all entrepreneurs evade taxes, as is always subliminally presented by politicians, it's necessary to resort to such inventive methods as in your case in order to get money from entrepreneurs and justify the audits.

Finally, the politicians are also happy if they have lots of taxpayers' money to spend and can be generous to their voters. That's why they also encourage these machinations.

I can only advise you to accept the payment, even if it is of an extortionate nature. There are simply too many loopholes in the law to be able to take legal action against it."

Laura nodded. They returned to the tax officials and agreed to their proposal.

"Our first priority is to act legally. Compliance with the law is the basis of a functioning state and also our most important personal goal," explained one of the tax officials.

"It is good that you comply with the requirement of legality and make the lump sum payment," added the other tax official.

Bitterness

"I don't understand why that bitchy brat is making such a fuss over a thousand."

The two tax officials were in their car driving back to the office.

"These entrepreneurs are all greedy, and they can never get enough. They have no social conscience," replied the other. "Just because we take one thousand from her, without having found fault, she immediately talks about illegality."

"Social justice means nothing to them."

"By the way, did you hear that? The allowance for our lunch won't be increased this year."

"What? That just can't be true!"

"I've done the maths. It'll cost us ten a year. In a hundred years that would be one thousand."

"Unbelievable, a thousand less in a hundred years. Where is the social justice in that?"

They stared at the street bitterly.

Redistribution

"I think it's good that the rich pay a greater proportion of their income as taxes," said Efia. "This increases the wealth of all."

Laura had met up for lunch with three friends with whom she had attended secondary school.

One of them, Efia, had completed her training as a social worker in the three years that had passed and was now working for the state social welfare office.

The second, Jala, had completed education as a chemical laboratory assistant and was now working for a plastics production company.

The third, Minda, had decided to study economics and philosophy.

"I've earned well in recent years with my computer consulting company," replied Laura, "and my tax rates have been correspondingly high.

With the money I paid because of the increased tax rates, I could have made further investments.

My blood pressure monitor costs a third less than those on the market. This saves a buyer a lot of money that he can spend on other things.

But in taking money away from me and thereby delaying production, the state is harming consumers because they now have to continue buying an expensive product and have less money for other expenses.

The state is also reducing the tax outcome of my company. If I had been able to invest the money, I could have produced more, had one more worker and paid more taxes.

High taxes are obviously a loss for everyone."

"But what about the people who don't need one of your blood pressure monitors?" asked Efia.

"What Laura says," replied Minda, "applies to the whole of society.

When the state takes money away from people, it prevents them from creating new value.

The prosperity we have today has been achieved because entrepreneurs like Laura have created new value. New products and services and cheaper products and services have been created.

By creating value, the poverty of the past has been eliminated.

This was not achieved by redistributing the wealth of past centuries.

If you only distribute existing wealth and, in addition, the state distributors in doing this need a large part for their payment, you cannot eradicate poverty.

Money is pushed back and forth by the state apparatus and largely used for self-sufficiency, instead of being used by entrepreneurs to create new value and therefore wealth for all.

This would be the same in the unrealistic case that the state apparatus itself doesn't need money. The money taken away still wouldn't be available for entrepreneurs, and they wouldn't be able to invest and create new value and wealth for all.

High taxes and redistribution ultimately make everyone poorer."

Social Justice

"It is considered socially just if rich people pay a larger share of their income in taxes, even if, as a side effect, the prosperity for all is obviously reduced and people become poorer as a result," interjected Efia.

"But that doesn't make sense if you take something from the richer ones and in the end the poorer ones have less," said Laura.

"Many people are happier when others lose more than they lose. They don't care that they lose themselves," replied Minda. "Envy is obviously disguised by the words 'social justice'.

Envy is often a motive, but who wants to admit that to himself or others? Social justice, on the other hand, is considered to be a noble motive."

"What's the definition of social justice?" asked Laura.

"The word 'social' before 'justice' seems to be just a catchword that can give any meaning to the concept of justice," she added. "Why do we even need to put a word before justice? After all, justice stands for itself."

"Social justice is actually always used as a protective term for actions. Anyone who criticises these actions is automatically be declared a bad person," replied Minda.

"Consider your case. You make an effort and develop a good blood pressure monitor. One day you will earn a lot of money with it and hand over fifty percent of your income to the state in tax.

Another person makes no effort and earns less. He therefore only gives ten percent of his income to the state in tax.

No one would dare to say that it's fair to punish effort and you should pay more taxes because of it.

So, you simply put the word 'social' in front of it and you get a new, seemingly acceptable form of justice, the so-called social justice, which approves of this injustice."

"One could call the justice of those who want to create something themselves and work to make their fortune 'natural justice'," said Jala.

"Social justice is therefore the justice of those who live by taking away from others what they themselves have created. It's the justice of politicians who stir up envy and promise to satisfy these demands, or the justice of simple muggers who rob someone."

"If you define it that way," replied Laura, "then natural justice is that form of justice that a child would feel without ever having thought theoretically about the concept. Social justice, on the other hand, is simply a concept that confuses and destroys the understanding of justice so much that it justifies every evil act."

New Ideas

The small steel door in the prison wall opened.

A judiciary official came out together with Flora.

Laura was already waiting outside the door.

The judiciary official looked at Flora with a stern face and said in a kind tone, "Don't do such nonsense again. Prison is no place for a young woman like you. I never want to see you here again."

"I don't think it was so bad," replied Flora, "and besides, we'd never have met otherwise."

She hugged the judiciary official and gave her a kiss on the cheek.

The judiciary official sighed and looked at Laura. "Please talk your sister out of such nonsense in the future."

Laura also sighed. "If it were that simple."

The judiciary official disappeared again behind the steel door in the prison wall.

Flora hugged Laura and also gave her a kiss on the cheek.

"I've used the time very profitably," said Flora. "I was able to meet some interesting people and I have already had some new project ideas."

Laura stared at her in surprise. Then she laughed out loud.

She hooked her arm into Flora's. "Come on, let's go eat, or did you even like the food in prison?"

Regulations

"You must place a sign here that says 'Exit'."

The official from the State Industrial Inspectorate was standing in Laura's factory workshop and pointed to the workshop door.

"But this is the only door to the workshop," said Laura.

"It doesn't matter," said the official, "this is prescribed in Section 231 of the Industrial Workshops Act.

Since the sign isn't yet up, you will be fined three hundred."

"I wasn't aware of that," replied Laura. "I'm going to hang up the sign, but I don't think it's appropriate that I've to pay a fine for this."

"Ignorance does not protect against punishment," the official replied with a cautionary look.

"It would have been useful if your colleague who was here a fortnight ago had pointed this out to me."

"He was only responsible for those measures which concern the first 200 Sections of the Industrial Workshops Act," the official replied indignantly. "One person cannot know the whole Industrial Workshops Act."

Ducks

Taio slowed down.

He and Laura were sitting together in his van. It was half past six in the evening. Both had stopped work earlier than normal that day because they wanted to go for a walk along the riverbank after dinner.

In front of them a family of ducks waddled across the road to a park. Apparently, they had been on the grass edge on the other side of the road before. There was a pond in the park a short distance from the road.

The mother duck went first, followed by six ducklings that could not yet fly. The drake turned towards the car and quacked angrily at it.

Laura and Taio laughed.

In the distance they saw a car coming. Laura got out and made a small turn to avoid the drake that was now croaking at her. She stood on the road to stop the oncoming car.

The driver stopped and yelled out, "What are you doing? Clear the road!"

"Can't you see! There are ducks crossing the road."

"What do I care?"

The driver honked.

The drake flew up startled and landed on the grass some thirty metres away. The mother duck and the ducklings ran on in panic.

Laura was angry. "What would you've done if the mother duck had flown away too? The ducklings wouldn't have known what to do."

"I don't care, just clear the road."

Laura did this and the car drove on with the engine howling.

Laura got back into the van.

"I know that ruthless guy," she said. "That's the official from the State Industrial Inspectorate who gave me trouble about the door sign."

"Unpleasant guy," replied Taio.

Laura looked at the pond. "Look," she said and put her hand on Taio's, "everything has turned out well in the end."

All the ducks had reached the pond and were now swimming around together.

They laughed at each other, and then they fell silent.

They were looking into each other's eyes and slowly leaning towards each other and a car behind them honked.

Startled, Taio put the van into gear and they drove on.

Free Animals

The official of the State Industrial Inspectorate was angry.

Normally he was already sitting in front of his television at half past six. However, this evening he needed to drive his car to the repair shop.

To make matters worse, he had had to brake because of some ducks.

He was always annoyed about animals living in the wild because they did not obey any rules. He was therefore convinced that wild animals should only live in a zoo. That would be the only way to give them a regulated existence governed by a set of rules laid down by a responsible state institution.

It's the same with people, he continued to himself. They also need rules like the animals in the zoo, and a director and a keeper to enforce those rules.

That is why entrepreneurs were anathema to him. He disliked people who wanted to shape their lives according to their free will and always wanted to implement new ideas. For him, they were like wild animals who did not live in a zoo.

It is impossible, he thought, that people can live according to their own free will with their only limitation being that they do not harm others.

I am truly a man of freedom, he thought, but freedom needs politicians to tell you what to do and state officials to make sure you do it.

A Favour

"I need a favour from you."

The head of the Employers' Association had come to the office of the senior ministerial customs officer. He sat down at the desk of the official vehemently without the customary greeting. As the table wobbled, some coffee spilled from the official's cup onto the saucer.

"We have a competitor who makes blood pressure monitors for non-medical purposes. He therefore pays no duty on the components he imports. I think that since these components could also be used for medical devices, customs duties could be charged."

The official looked at him bored. "I'm sure something could be done."

He stood up and turned to the shelf behind his desk, which contained a number of law books.

He chose one of them.

Then he put it on the table and opened it.

He tore out a page and carefully folded it together. Then he placed it under the wobbling table leg.

He put the law book back, sat down and sluggishly remarked, "This will cost you eight thousand."

"Fine," said the head of the Employers' Association and left the room without a greeting.

Arbitrariness

Laura looked astonished at the customs notice in her hand.

It contained a customs claim for membranes which she had purchased from a foreign manufacturer.

To begin with, Laura had not had to pay any duty for the membranes. But now the membranes were listed in the customs notice as medical devices for which customs duties had to be paid.

The customs claim doubled the price which she had originally paid to the foreign manufacturer.

Laura knew that medical membranes were subject to customs duties. However, her membranes were not used for any medical purpose and no duty was to pay for such membranes. There was no legal reason to pay this duty.

She thought for a moment and called Taio. He imported some of his printers from abroad and probably already had experience in working with customs.

"Hello," he called happily into the phone, and she realised that she too was pleased to hear his voice.

They chatted for some time, then she told him about the customs officers' procedure.

He thought for a moment. "The only advice I can give you is to ask the lawyer. It stinks when the customs office suddenly changes its mind."

After a short chat, they ended the conversation. Laura leaned back smiling and closed her eyes briefly.

Then she sighed, sat up and called the lawyer.

Political Support

"The Minister for Economic Affairs is coming," murmured one visitor.

Laura was standing behind a table at the edge of a large hall full of such tables.

In front of her stood her blood pressure monitor. Some brochures with a description of the device were also placed on the table.

The State Agency for the Support of Start-up Foundation had organised an event where young entrepreneurs could present their products free of charge.

Laura had been contacted and had taken up the opportunity.

When a company was founded, the officials of the Admissions Office had to fill in a form for the State Enterprise Coordination Office.

For its part, the State Enterprise Coordination Office informed the Central State Enterprise Support Unit.

The Central State Enterprise Support Unit then passed the information on to the State Agency for the Support of General Enterprise Foundation.

The State Agency for the Support of General Enterprise Foundation then informed the State Agency for the Support of Start-up Foundation in a specific case like Laura's.

This is how Laura's company data came to be included in the file of the State Agency for the Support of Start-up Foundation.

Laura already had three employees and the business had started well. However, she had decided to take part in the event anyway, as she hoped to make new customer contacts.

The Minister for Economic Affairs also attended the event. His position in the hall was easily recognisable among the crowd of members of various state agencies, journalists and photographers who surrounded him.

This crowd was now moving towards Laura's table, as the visitor, who had just stood in front of Laura's neighbouring table, had noticed.

At Laura's neighbouring table on the left, in the direction from which the minister came, a young man in unkempt clothing was standing.

Laura had already spoken with him. His product was software designed to prevent criminally infiltrated malware from encrypting user data for blackmailing purposes.

Laura had been repeatedly confronted with this issue in her work as a computer consultant and was familiar with the technical content of the problem. During her conversation with the young man she had gained a good impression of his competence and the quality of his product.

She had asked him to give her a business card, as she had planned to ask her employee, whom she had hired for her computer consulting company, to consider recommending the product to her customers after a closer examination.

The group with the Minister had now almost reached Laura and her neighbour. The Minister was heading towards the two tables with a grin. The young man from the neighbouring table stepped forward to greet him.

The Minister just passed the young man who was reaching out his hand and continued to smile as he approached Laura.

The crowd surrounding the Minister pushed the young man roughly aside. He stumbled and pulled his table to the floor with a loud rumble.

Before Laura could come to the young man's aid, she was already trapped in the Minister's crowd.

The Minister ignored the rumble and grinningly pulled Laura's hand towards him. He held it for a minute in the photographers' flashlight storm.

"I am delighted to see here once again an example of how successful our government support programmes are, which specifically support and motivate young women to start a business."

"I've not submitted an application for government fundi..."

"What interesting product do you have there?" The Minister kept grinning at her.

"A blood pressure monitor that espec..."

"Ah, very innovative, and the company is doing well?"

"I've had trouble with customs recently becau..."

"Yes, customs duties are an important thing." The Minister turned to the journalists with a serious expression. "They are important for social justice."

He went on grinning and the crowd followed him.

Laura helped the young man to set up his table again and rearranged his brochures.

Free Trade and Cooperation

Laura had met up with Jala, Efia and Minda once again for lunch.

She had told them about the surprising change in her customs assessment.

"For my customers, the collection of the duty is definitely detrimental," said Laura. "It makes the blood pressure monitor more expensive."

"Tariffs are always about clientele policy," said Minda. "One group benefits at the expense of another."

"Can't the overall benefits outweigh the disadvantages then?" asked Efia.

"No," replied Minda. "On the whole, it is always a disadvantage.

The enormous growth in productivity in both manufacturing and services over the last 250 years has been in large part due to the increasing division of labour.

In the past, most people produced their own food and clothing, for example. However, this has been replaced by strong specialisations. Everyone now produces what he does best.

Laura is a good example, she makes her blood pressure monitor because she is good at it, but she buys other things like food and clothes.

Of course, the division of labour and cooperation between people always went beyond the borders of states because it brought great benefits to the people.

Both are the basis of our prosperity.

Of course, there have always been people who wanted to eliminate competition in their favour. The easiest way to do this across the borders of individual states has always been through customs duties.

The rulers themselves earned directly from the customs duties and at the same time could be sure of the favour of influential groups. For those groups that were favoured by the ruler, this was the easiest way to eliminate competition. This still has not changed until today.

This was always a disadvantage for the majority of the population, as the better products became more expensive and people either paid more for them or had to resort to the lower quality products. This still has not changed until today.

This was also always a disadvantage for those groups who wanted to sell products to other countries themselves, because they were also charged customs duties in return. This still has not changed until today, either.

In Laura's case, too, the reason for these unexpected customs regulations seems to be the desire to prevent competition in the marketplace. This is to the detriment of customers and to the advantage of individuals who have good connections to state institutions."

"But it would be best for the government to promote free trade if it makes people more prosperous," said Jala.

"Politicians are guided by the interests of the clientele that's most important to them," said Minda. "This is a common abuse of power by the state, in which individual groups gain advantages to the detriment of others."

Free Trade by Free People

"I see this as quite separate from the benefits of free trade that you just pointed out, Minda," said Laura.

"It's fundamentally wrong that officials and politicians can tell me who I can trade with.

As a responsible citizen, I must be able to trade with whomever I like. It isn't as if I trade in weapons or prohibited substances.

No outsider has any right to tell me from whom I buy the rubber membranes.

The fact that an outsider exerts influence, either through direct violence or through politicians and officials, is a pure abuse of power.

These trade restrictions can't be justified by any moral concepts of free people. This is the morality of slaveholders who presume to interfere with the individual rights of individuals.

As a free human being, only I am entitled to decide which free human being I talk with, spend my time or exchange ideas and goods with.

Free action and thus free trade are my fundamental inherent human rights."

Corrupt Trade

"You can be sure that the sudden change of opinion by state customs officials was caused by corruption," said the lawyer.

Laura was sitting in the lawyer's office as they discussed further procedures regarding the customs duty on the rubber membranes.

"The only way you can fight it is to use the same means as your opponents."

"I just want to buy the membranes. Is nothing possible without corruption and breaking the law when dealing with state institutions?" Laura looked at the lawyer angrily.

"In your case, the state customs officers changed their mind spontaneously, so you can be sure that there is no law governing the case. The officials have interpreted the matter freely.

You're not breaking any law by importing your membranes duty free.

But you won't be able to avoid resorting to the same means to influence these people's opinions."

"Can I even afford this?"

"I think so. We'll just have to find a hole at the lowest level."

Laura sighed and shook her head.

"Customs duties are always a form of corruption, whether legal or illegal," said the lawyer. "One group enriches itself with customs duties at the expense of another.

If the group is influential enough, it can get politicians to put a tariff into law and make it legal.

The group is thus forcing others to buy its products at a higher price because it can block the cheaper products through customs.

In the final analysis, the whole thing is nothing more than corruption cast into law."

"The only way to prevent the state from abusing its power to act is obviously not to give state institutions the right to intervene in trade relations," said Laura.

"That would be the ideal case," said the lawyer.

Derby

"How do you think I look now?" asked the senior ministerial customs officer.

The head of the Employers' Association had called the senior ministerial customs officer and had confronted him with the fact that Laura was still importing the membranes without paying customs duties.

The senior ministerial customs officer had then called the head of the airport customs office.

"An older colleague let the membranes pass as rubber rags. He claimed that he was not informed about the matter with the membranes," replied the head of the airport customs office.

"Didn't you involve him?" asked the senior ministerial customs officer.

"No."

"How should I explain this? How do you imagine this is to happen now?"

"Well," mused the head of the airport customs office, "I think ..."

The senior ministerial customs officer heard the beeping of an electric alarm clock in the background.

"I'm sorry," said the head of the airport customs office, "today is the derby of the Second Regional Football League. I've got to get home in time to watch it on TV."

He hung up.

The senior ministerial customs officer threw the receiver angrily back on the phone.

Nothing like this had ever happened to him before.

He had never forgotten to get home in time for the derby of the Second Regional Football League on TV.

He hastily took his briefcase and left his office in a hurry.

Altruism

"You also have to take on obligations to others," interjected Laura's mother.

It was the weekend, and Laura's and Flora's parents had invited them to dinner.

Laura had told them that her company was flourishing and that she had already hired three employees. Flora had recently successfully completed several trading projects as well.

Their mother had told them about a cousin who was looking for a job as a secretary and had asked Laura to hire her.

Laura refused, because she currently did not need anyone with this qualification in her company.

"What obligation should I have to give others what I have earned," asked Laura.

"Why should I give others what I've created or will create, so that they can live their lives as they wish?

Why should I, just because I've created something, not be able to shape my life according to my own ideas?"

"You let Flora live with you for free," said her mother.

"Yes, because I care about Flora and I enjoy having her, not because of any vague altruistic obligations that are being imposed on me."

"You should give your cousin a job in your company. She needs it. It is your moral duty to give something to her. In addition, you're related and you're an entrepreneur."

"That's a strange morality you're advocating," said Laura. "Those who own less have the right to access the property of those who own more. Those who own something are the slaves of those who own less.

This is a robber's morality, a morality of arbitrariness and violence. Someone has the right to take something from someone else just because the person concerned has more of it."

Responsibility and Coercion

"You also have to take responsibility for others, not just for yourself," said Laura's mother. "You have responsibility for your cousin."

Laura looked at her.

"Who but myself should be responsible for what I do?

Just as I'm responsible for my actions, others are responsible for their actions.

Just as others are not responsible for my actions, I'm not responsible for their actions.

It isn't my right or my duty to take responsibility for others, neither spiritually nor materially.

Nor is it the right or duty of others to take spiritual or material responsibility for my actions.

Of course, I can support others in their actions, but only at my request and with the consent of those concerned. Anything else would be coercion, and I see no justification for it.

Such coercion has its justification only in exercising power over the concerned, for the latter this is pure arbitrariness.

What you call responsibility is only an attempt to give arbitrary coercion the appearance of a noble act."

Imposition

"I could use the help of our cousin," said Flora. "I want to sell a larger quantity of jumpers in the near future. If there's a profit in it, we could share it."

"What if you don't make a profit?" asked her mother.

"Then there is nothing to distribute," replied Flora.

"But you can't do that to your cousin, then she wouldn't get any earnings for her work."

"Me neither." Flora smiled at her. "That's the risk with projects like this."

"I can't suggest that to your cousin, it would be an imposition."

Flora laughed. "I put up with it myself."

"I think it's an imposition that we have to solve a cousin's problems at dinner," interjected their father. "Flo, pass the potatoes over here, please."

"You and Laura should eat another portion before you lose weight on the job."

They smiled at him and took some more food.

Innovation and Joy

Laura was sitting in her office and looking at a paper in front of her, on which were listed the wishes of the Judo Association.

The Judo Association had already bought some of her blood pressure monitors. The head of the association had called Laura a few days ago and expressed satisfaction with their performance.

During the conversation, Laura had noticed that it might be of interest to the athletes to record further readings of various body functions during training. There was also an interest in making the device even smaller and handier.

Laura had then agreed with the head of the Judo Association to visit him to discuss further details regarding the desired features of the equipment.

She had done that today, and the list was now in front of her.

She set out to draw up a plan of how the wishes could be realised technically. At the same time, she considered how long this would probably take and what costs would be involved.

After three hours she had drawn up a rough plan which seemed realistic to her.

There were so many things to try out, develop and implement that she would have loved to start right away. The upcoming development work made her feel euphoric.

The idea of developing something new always inspired her. Thinking about it, putting it into practice in a real component or in software, trying it out and improving it – she loved these phases of development, in which the product matured in front of her eyes.

Since the blood pressure monitor was now selling well, she had raised enough money to finance its further development.

The daily well-rehearsed work in production and sales was being carried out by three employees. As planned, she would hire a part-time worker who could help with packaging and shipping. This would enable her to devote a larger part of her time to the further development of the device.

She leaned back contentedly in her armchair and thought how good it was that she had earned enough money to be able to afford the development work.

Independent Research

Laura nodded to the small group of people that Minda had just introduced to her.

She was in Minda's flat. Minda had recently started writing freelance articles for a business journal. To celebrate the occasion, she had invited some people over. The small flat was crowded, and the visitors chatted in small groups.

"You have similar jobs. You're both exploring new things," the hostess said to a young man in the group.

"What are you researching?" asked the young man.

"I'd rather call it development," replied Laura. "I've developed a blood pressure monitor, and I'm in the process of implementing a major enhancement."

"Interesting," said the young man. "At which institute is your project running?"

"I do it myself," said Laura.

"Who's going to pay for this?"

"Myself, I earned the necessary start-up money as a computer consultant and now I sell the blood pressure monitors. It's going pretty well."

"But this isn't independent research if you're dependent on the market," said the young man.

"Why? I'm completely independent and free to develop what I want. Of course, I sell the devices and earn money with them. After all, that's the goal of my work."

The young man looked at her sceptically.

"How do you finance your research?" asked Laura.

"I'm independent. I work at the university and get my money from the state."

Laura nodded and thought for a moment. "That means you have an account with taxpayers' money that you can access freely?"

"Of course not. I've submitted a research project," said the young man. "That was approved. With the money, I can now work freely."

"But then who approved it?" asked Laura.

"Older, more experienced professors, men and women of recognised professional competence."

"But then you depend on those people to approve what you're allowed to do?"

"They know what you need and what to research and have the experience and knowledge to do it. In a few years' time, when I've built up a sufficient reputation, I'll also be part of such an assessment group and will make funding decisions together with others."

He looked at her proudly.

"This means that you now do what older men and women tell you to do, and your aim is to be able to tell a younger person what to do when you're older yourself."

Laura looked at him smiling. "This isn't what I imagine by freedom to carry out development work. Freedom to me is when I decide on my actions and don't let others do it for me."

Night Watchman State

"What makes you think that we don't need a state?"

A young man, who had joined the group, addressed Laura.

"I never said that," replied Laura. "Just because I don't want to be patronised by employees of state institutions doesn't mean that I don't believe we need state institutions."

"What task do you see for the state then?" asked a young woman.

"I believe that the state should ensure the safety of people and make sure that contracts are respected."

"Military, police and judiciary," said another young man.

"Yes, I think we need these institutions," replied Laura. "But otherwise? We're people who think for ourselves, and the state institutions are not beings in their own right but are formed by people who work there.

Why should people working in state institutions be allowed to determine how people outside these institutions should live their lives?

What should distinguish these people who work in state institutions in such a way that they supposedly know better than other people for themselves what those should and should not do?"

"You mean the state should be like a night watchman in a medieval town," said a young woman. "He was paid by the citizens to ensure their safety. But he couldn't tell them what to do in everyday life."

"A good example," said Laura, "yes, a night watchman state. A state that is democratically empowered by its citizens to protect their rights.

State institutions are not there to grant rights to citizens.

State institutions are there to defend the rights of citizens."

The State a Being

"You say, 'state institutions are not beings'. But there are still state interests," interjected a young woman. "A statesman once said, 'Ask not what the state can do for you, but what you can do for the state'."

"The state institutions are formed by people and the so-called interests of the state are no more than the interests of the people who run the state institutions," replied Minda, who had joined the discussion.

"The state is not a being with its own will or interests.

Only individuals can think and act. When three people form a group, they are three thinking beings. There is then no group as a fourth thinking being."

"We are all the state," said the young woman.

"Then I don't understand what you're saying at all," said Laura. "We all have our own interests and intentions. Why should the interests and intentions of others be more important to me than my own, and why should my interests be more important to others?

This is only confusing and leads to the fact that nobody can do anything according to his will anymore. This is a slave organisation, where in the end only the will of the so-called heads of state counts."

"Historically, these have always been the roots of so-called state interests," said Minda. "A ruler or strong lobby group dictates something and says it is the state interest or the general interest.

In this way, the interests of the individual are automatically declared to be of lesser value, and he is degraded to the status of the recipient of orders in the name of the fictitious general interest."

Public Research

"The efficient use of state research funding and the guarantee of economically unaffected research are our most honourable tasks."

The head of the commission looked at his two assessors, a professor of experimental physics and a professor of theoretical physics, who nodded their approval.

The three of them had the task of making a recommendation to the State Funding Agency for Basic Research in Physics. They headed physics institutes at three different state universities.

On the basis of their recommendations, government grants were awarded once every six months for basic research projects in physics.

"Four applications have been received. I've asked a young member of my staff to evaluate them in terms of their content. He'll also take the minutes during the meeting."

He pointed to a young man who was sitting at a small table at the edge of the room who nodded his head and greeted.

"According to the ranking of my assistant, the applications are referred to as application one to application four in order to treat them anonymously and to ensure the objectivity of the award.

My assistant said that application one was outstandingly innovative and by far the best of all applications.

I therefore propose that we allocate eighty percent of the funding to application one, ten percent to application two and ten percent to application three."

The male assessor leafed through the documents. "Application four is from a staff member of mine. My institute would then get nothing. We were not considered for the last two rounds of awards either."

"But you didn't ask for anything there," said the head of the commission.

"Nevertheless, it would be unfair if we were to get nothing again now. We have to buy expensive equipment for our experiments. I suggest eighty percent of the total for application four."

"Even if we do theoretical physics, ten percent is too little for us, so I'm asking for twenty percent for application three, which comes from my institute," added the female assessor.

"But then there is nothing left for application two from my institute," said the head of the commission.

"Since you've already earned so many merits for research, I'll make every effort to ensure that you receive the Grand National Merit Badge for Science," replied the female assessor.

"A very good idea, I'll fully support you," said the male assessor.

"Thank you very much for your appreciation," said the head of the commission happily. "It has therefore been decided that eighty percent of the amount will go to application four and twenty percent to application three."

"What happens to application one?" asked the young assistant.

"To which institute does the applicant actually belong?" asked the female assessor.

"The request came from a PhD student who is not assigned to any institute," replied the young assistant.

"Application one gets nothing," interjected the head of the commission brusquely.

"We cannot distribute our scarce resources arbitrarily.

The efficient use of state research funding and the guarantee of economically unaffected research are our most honourable tasks."

The two assessors nodded in agreement.

Way Clear for the Minister

"I can only deliver the spare parts after 6 pm the traffic jams won't have dispersed before then anyway."

Laura was sitting in her office on the phone with Taio.

A sensor on a 3D printer had failed and production was therefore only two-thirds of the usual capacity.

Production was actually supposed to be running at full speed at the moment because the order situation was very good. Laura had already ordered a fourth 3D printer, but it was going to take another two weeks to deliver it, so the current failure of one printer was all the more stressful.

Taio had the spare part in stock and had left immediately after Laura's first call. She had been expecting him at 1 pm with the spare part, but he was still stuck in traffic.

The Foreign Minister of another country was in the city and had attended an exhibition and reception with his host, the domestic Foreign Minister. The police uninhibitedly blocked the respective routes on which they were travelling through the city, which had brought traffic to a standstill.

"Fine," said Laura, "I'll be here."

Laura calculated that she would have to work until 2 am for the next three nights to make up for the several hours of lost production caused by the Foreign Ministers. During the night she would have to work alone without her staff. It would therefore take that long to catch up on the backlog.

She wondered whether it would be possible to get the state institutions to pay for the damage caused by them.

She shook her head briefly and continued working.

Free Creation and Joy

Laura yawned and looked contentedly at the blood pressure monitors packed in front of her on a pallet.

It was 2 am, and she decided to go to bed as planned. By 7 am she would need to be back in the factory workshop.

She was satisfied with the day's performance. She hadn't worried about the cause of the delay, the roadblocks. They were simply a problem she had just solved.

The capacity utilisation of her company was very good, and she was proud of this success.

She looked with pleasure at the machines in the factory workshop and the pallets filled with finished blood pressure monitors.

Despite her tiredness, the thought of her work made her happy.

I love my work, she told herself with a smile. Every single action and every thought.

I love to develop solutions to technical problems.

I love to work independently according to my will, taking my own responsibility and at my own risk.

I love to create something.

Yawning and satisfied, she made her way home.

Ministerial Priorities

The Foreign Minister looked satisfied in the mirror.

He was standing in his bedroom and going through the events of the day. He had achieved a lot.

It had taken him a lot of effort in the last few weeks to reach his goal. He had even incurred the displeasure of some ministerial colleagues. But he had not given up because the matter was important to him.

His success proved him right.

The board with the logo of the Ministry of Foreign Affairs on the main building would not become smaller than the boards of other ministries after the renovations.

It had all started two months ago with a decision to give all ministries a new look.

It was common practice to do this at regular intervals.

This allowed taxpayers' money to be allocated to advertising agencies that were close to the parties currently in power. In the event of a change of government, this was a matter of course. If there were no elections or change of government for a longer period of time, it had to be done anyway.

The annoying thing had been that the board with the new logo had proportions that did not fit in the place of the old board. It would have covered some windows on the front of the Ministry of Foreign Affairs.

The advertising agency that created the logo did not want to change the proportions of the logo for artistic reasons. They proposed to reduce the size of the board proportionally.

The Foreign Minister could not allow this.

The board on his ministry would have been smaller than those that hung in front of other ministries, even though his ministry, he was quite certain, was the most important.

Therefore, he had demanded that the proportions of the logo were changed. The advertising agency, as they stated, was opposed to this for artistic reasons.

But when it was promised that they would receive the same amount of taxpayers' money for the second draft as for the first, they agreed to the modification.

Now the board on his ministry was no smaller than those on others.

He was proud of his success.

The Foreign Minister recalled that another foreign colleague would be visiting tomorrow.

The next moment he shook his head in annoyance. That had already happened today. He remembered the quail eggs at lunch.

The urgent settlement of the affair with the board had cost him so much energy that he had almost forgotten the state visit. He could no longer remember the content of the talks exactly. Nothing of any importance, he thought to himself.

He was happy to spend the next day quietly in the office again.

Then he would finally be able to read the report he had received from the State Visits Department three days ago. It contained a description of the country from which today's state guest had come.

He also decided to look at the globe in his office to see where the country actually was.

Just Like Old Times

Minda had just phoned Laura to invite her to dinner on Saturday evening.

Laura told her that she had worked three times until 2 am because of the traffic jams caused by the state visit.

"It's just like old times," said Minda. "If a ruler wanted to travel freely with a fast carriage, a farmer's hay cart was simply tipped over, no matter whether the cart broke down or the hay fell into a stream flowing beside it.

Today, ministers are also taking this right to clear the way."

"But nothing can justify that," said Laura. "There is no reason why the work of these people should be more important than that of other citizens.

After all, they're only employees of a state institution, paid by the taxpayer, and a meeting of foreign ministers is not an emergency situation such as a rescue operation either."

"You're right," replied Minda, "but the ministers are simply taking this right, as they did in the past, no matter what damage they do.

A very commonplace, banal case of the state abuse of power."

Cooperation with Laura

Laura and Taio were sitting with Minda in her flat. It was Saturday evening, they were talking and waiting for the other guests to arrive.

Minda had invited Laura, Jala and Efia. Since plus ones were also included in the invitation, Laura had asked Taio if he wanted to come along.

"It's hard to imagine how many people are involved in making my blood pressure monitor," said Laura. "I could give thousands of different examples."

"Give an example that isn't immediately obvious," said Taio.

Laura pondered briefly.

"For example, a manufacturer of grinding machines which are used to produce gears for transmissions helps me. His customers make the gears that are then used for the gearboxes of tractors. The tractors are used by other people to harvest the wood that's a basic material for the top of my office desk, and so on. Until the table is in my office, many companies and people are still involved.

The grinding machine manufacturer contributes to the production of my blood pressure monitor."

"He doesn't even know you exist," said Taio. "All that matters to him is that people want to make gears with his grinders."

"Yes, I cooperate with many people in the manufacture of my blood pressure monitor, to our mutual satisfaction, without us knowing about each other."

Cooperation and Society

"What you've described is the foundation of our society, which is based on the free market economy," said Minda.

"All people are networked through the division of labour and thus form society. In this way, everyone contributes something to the interaction of the society, even though he doesn't know most of the other members personally.

Society is a vast voluntary cooperation based on the idea that everyone wants to achieve the greatest benefit for himself and must therefore help others to meet their needs.

Almost nobody knows the people he helps. The manufacturer of the grinding machines has no idea about your existence, but nevertheless his work makes it possible for you to sell your blood pressure monitors.

Society functions in this way voluntarily because everyone benefits from it.

There is no need for any coordinating power in the form of politicians or state institutions.

The manufacturer of the grinding machines produces them because he wants to earn money with them. He automatically helps you with it, without a politician having to give him an order for it.

The free market economy or, in other words, capitalism is the necessary but also sufficient basis of our society."

Cooperation and Equality

"The manufacturer of the grinding machines helps me as much as he helps you," said Taio. "By making his grinding machines, he's helping both of us, without having the possibility of favouring or discriminating against either of us."

"Yes, it's a voluntary cooperation where it isn't possible to favour or discriminate against anyone," said Laura.

"This is a beautiful and essential aspect of capitalist society," said Minda. "Everyone helps the other without prejudice or exclusion.

The manufacturer of the grinding machines will help you without knowing you. If you have political views that he doesn't share, it doesn't matter. If he doesn't agree with you because of your appearance, it doesn't matter. If he doesn't agree with you because of your religion, it doesn't matter.

Whatever the reason he doesn't agree with you, it doesn't matter. His grinding machines would still contribute to your success in making your blood pressure monitor. He cannot prevent that he automatically contributes to your prosperity.

Discrimination and exclusion only ever arise when politicians disrupt this voluntary cooperation on behalf of the state.

Whether through customs duties, regulations or fomenting nationalist or religious prejudice, in the end, all they care about is disrupting cooperation in order to create advantages for certain groups. In voluntary cooperation under capitalism, no one needs the intervention of politicians.

Disruption of voluntary cooperation by politicians is always associated with exclusion and discrimination, as the only way to do so is to introduce rules that favour or discriminate against individual groups.

A capitalist society is based on voluntary cooperation and knows no discrimination or exclusion. All people are treated equally."

Personal Cooperation

Minda went into the kitchen.

"The best thing that has happen to me," said Taio, "is that our cooperation has not remained anonymous."

Laura looked at him.

Then she smiled mischievously and said, "If it's always so nice to get to know your suppliers personally, maybe I should try to meet other suppliers in person as well."

"I think this is a very bad idea," replied Taio laughing.

"Do you have a better one?" asked Laura.

"I'm thinking more of a very personal cooperation, just between us," said Taio.

They laughed at each other, and then they fell silent.

Taio took her hand and she smiled at him.

They were looking into each other's eyes and slowly leaning towards each other and the doorbell rang.

"Please open the door for the others," called Minda from the kitchen.

Wealthiness

Jala and Efia had arrived. Efia had also brought a young man with her.

They introduced themselves to each other. Efia's companion was a young functionary of a political party that advocated the redistribution of private wealth by state functionaries.

Efia had told him about the four friends' conversation about high taxes and justice. So, in the evening there was a discussion about these topics.

"Doesn't it bother you to get rich?" asked the young functionary looking at Laura. "Having a very imbalanced income distribution is bad for society."

"Why should that bother me?" asked Laura.

"I've earned my own property through my own work. I'm happy about it and proud of it. Everyone who buys my blood pressure monitors does so voluntarily because he has a personal benefit from it.

I'm not rich yet, but I would be happy to be. It would be a sign that I've worked successfully, which would give me satisfaction.

My customers benefit from my work. They have a blood pressure monitor that gives them a benefit, otherwise they wouldn't have bought it.

In addition, my device is cheaper than those of the competition, which has saved customers money and increased their prosperity.

If I became rich, it would only mean that I've benefited a great many people and increased their prosperity.

Moreover, wealthiness also means financial independence and therefore freedom. I find that very desirable.

Sure, there will be people who own less than I do, but that isn't something I'm responsible for. I have never been interested in talk of envy."

Wealthiness and Prosperity

"What Laura says is basically true in a market economy," said Minda.

"Those entrepreneurs who create the greatest benefit for their customers will be the richest. After all, this benefit is the only motivation for customers to buy.

Look at the richest entrepreneurs in the world. None of them were born rich, but they all benefited their customers so much that they became rich.

An evenly distributed income, except for a few rich people, can only be found in poor countries where politicians deprive people of the opportunity to build up a fortune.

These are the countries where the market economy is suppressed. There, everyone is equally poor. Except for some politicians and their circle of friends, who enrich themselves by concentrating the few assets on themselves.

The more wealthy entrepreneurs there are in a country with a market economy, the more wealth has been created and the richer all the people in the country are."

Joy and Greed

It was late in the evening. Laura and Taio had already left as they had to get up very early. Their businesses were going very well, and they had a lot to do. Efia's companion had also just said goodbye.

"Strange," said Jala, "he has now stormed away angrily. He seemed so bitter all the time during our conversation. Somehow quite the opposite of Laura."

"I'm glad he left," said Efia. "I don't want to see him anymore, bitter as he is."

"If you have a certain basic attitude, this is usually reflected in your behaviour," said Minda. "There is a big difference in the basic attitude of Laura and that young functionary.

The young functionary is a member of a political party that wants to take people's property away from them in order to distribute it among other people according to the will of the party leaders.

The behaviour of such organisations is quite different from that of Laura. The people there stir up envy in order to increase the number of their followers. They talk negatively about those who want to create something or have created something for themselves.

They claim that it is unfair if those who have generated income own more and all those who own less are disadvantaged.

But this also influences the entire personal behaviour of these people, as can be seen with the young functionary.

If you are always talking negatively about others, always stirring up envy and claiming that those who want to create something are unfair, you get a bitter attitude like that young man.

Officials of such a party are not happy people, they only appear in public in a threatening or accusing manner.

They don't want to create anything themselves, they just want to take something from others, like robbers. They're driven by envy and greed for the wealth that others have created for themselves.

It is no coincidence that the young functionary is so embittered.

People like Laura, who see the free market economy or, in other words, capitalism as their basis for action, are people who want to create something.

They want to act creatively and create something new on the basis of voluntary cooperation with other people.

They don't want to take something away from others.

To create something new in voluntary cooperation with others is the joyful basic idea of capitalism.

Whatever the new is. In Laura's case, for example, this includes her service, where she looks after the computer systems of small entrepreneurs and the production of her blood pressure monitors.

That's why people like Laura are happy people. They want to create something in voluntary cooperation with others. They don't want to take anything away from others, no matter whether they own a company or work as employees in a company.

The workers in Laura's company, with whom I spoke last week, have exactly the same creative, cheerful attitude.

Capitalism is a cheerful, positive system of creation, a system of optimism, a system of the joy of creation and creative imagination.

It's no coincidence that Laura is such a cheerful person."

Collective Freedom

On the way home the young functionary thought about his visit to Minda. He was in a bad mood and was annoyed by the other guests and especially Minda.

He detested people like Laura, who wanted to shape their lives according to their own ideas.

The only correct way for people to shape their lives, he thought, is for the collective of people to decide what the individual should do.

Democratic socialism is the only correct form of society, he continued to himself. Nobody should have the right to decide on their own and selfishly about the path of life, as Laura does.

The majority of people should decide how Laura should live her life. Only then are people truly free.

The goal that people are truly free, he thought, is achieved through democratic socialism. No one must then be allowed to make selfish decisions for and about themselves, they must do what others want. That is true freedom.

This can be improved in the future, he thought. Millions of people cannot vote and know about every detail. You have to form a committee which prepares the decisions. Yes, a central committee, a central committee that makes these collective decisions.

Then everyone would be truly free and at the same time the state system would be well-organised.

Of course, decision making in such a committee was not always easy either. He knew that from his party meetings.

You can still optimise the whole thing, he thought. There must be a secretary to prepare the decisions.

In fact, the secretary actually has a management function, like a director, or rather a director-general.

Yes, it is a General Secretary, who will then take the democratic-socialist, collective decisions.

This is the right position for me, to be General Secretary of the Central Committee. This is a position that I can handle like no other.

"Yes," he said out loud, "I am ready to take democratic-socialist, collective decisions as General Secretary. All people would then be truly free and at the same time the state would be well-organised because I would make all decisions for them."

Egoists like this Laura, who believe they can live according to their own ideas, must then subordinate themselves to the democratic-socialist, collective decisions I make. Then all people would be truly free.

Proudly he looked at his reflection in a shop window he was just passing by.

The Trade Unionist

"You can't forbid your workers to talk to me."

The union official was standing in Laura's office and looking at her angrily.

"You're right," replied Laura in a friendly tone. "I don't want that either."

"Well, stop work now and send the people to me."

"Why should I do that?" asked Laura. "People are now working as we agreed in our contract and getting their pay. If they want to talk to you, they'll do so in their spare time."

"You're tyrannising your workers," cried the trade unionist.

A worker who had just come into the office laughed. "I don't feel bullied, I really like working here."

"We've taken down far more powerful exploiters than you," cried the union official and left the office.

Laura and the worker looked at each other in surprise and continued their work.

Bitterness

The union official was walking angrily from Laura's office to his car.

The reason for his anger was his car. He was not thinking about the conversation at Laura's office.

His car was a union company car. A middle-class sedan, which he had newly received and had been driving for three years.

At that time, he had been promised that he would receive a large SUV after these three years.

The day before, he had been informed that he would receive the promised wagon in just under four weeks and not, as originally agreed, in three days.

The union's district group had postponed the signing of the leasing contract for three weeks in order to save money.

The sumptuous buffet at the last meeting of the district officials had been more expensive than planned. The three-week postponement of the leasing contract was one of the measures taken to save expenses.

The union official considered the three-week waiting period particularly unfair, as he had not attended the last meeting of the district officials.

At that time, he had been on holiday to a five-star hotel on a palm-fringed beach, where there was a sumptuous buffet every day.

However, he had not really enjoyed the sumptuous buffet in the hotel, as he could not stop thinking of the one at the meeting of the district officials that he had missed due to his holiday.

Now he also had to wait three weeks for his large SUV.

As he walked, he thought bitterly that even in the trade union there was no social justice.

Emergency Call

"Stay calm and wait until we send someone."

Laura was standing in the dark not far from her factory workshop.

After a dinner with Taio, she had come back to work again.

She had wanted to work out and draw in detail a design improvement of a component of the blood pressure monitor, which she had been thinking about for the last few days.

But when she had arrived at her factory workshop, the light was on. In front of it was a delivery van with the doors of the loading bay open.

Obviously, there were burglars in the workshop. She had called the emergency number for the police and was now waiting according to their instructions.

Two men were pulling a handcart out of the workshop, on which a 3D printer and a computer stood. It looked as if they were about to load the machines into the van.

Laura thought about what she should do. She was physically inferior to the men, but if she did nothing, the men would drive away with her machines. The damage would be great and would ruin her company.

Although she was insured against minor thefts, she could not afford insurance against weeks of production downtime.

She took her big hand lamp out of the car. Standing concealed behind her car, she directed its powerful beam at the two men from a distance of forty metres.

Then she shouted, "Stop and don't move! Police."

She was getting ready to run away, but she was lucky.

The two men reacted as she had hoped. They jumped into their car and raced away without having loaded anything.

She spent the next hour on the spot waiting for the police. She did not dare to approach the workshop as she did not know if there were other burglars in it.

When the police still had not arrived an hour later, she carefully approached the workshop and was relieved to find that she was alone. In the meantime, another hour had passed.

The damage was less than she had feared. The gate lock was ruined, but the men had not touched anything except for one 3D printer and the computer. They had loaded the two devices onto the handcart without causing any major damage.

She pulled the handcart into the workshop and started to set up the equipment again. For a moment she considered calling Taio or Flora. But then she decided not to do so because of the time and the fact that she would not need any help to set up the equipment.

When she finished setting up and connecting the two devices, it was 1 am.

Since the workshop could no longer be locked and repairing the gate in the middle of the night did not seem to make sense, she decided to spend the night on site.

She parked her car in front of the gate and fell asleep in it shortly afterwards.

The police had not appeared.

Priorities

"A break-in was reported here?"

Laura was just opening a package of externally produced circuit boards when the police officers entered the factory workshop.

The policemen looked at her and her workers questioningly. It was 11 am.

"Yes, I reported it," replied Laura. "It was an emergency call at about 10 pm yesterday evening."

"We don't know anything about that," said one policeman. "We didn't arrive on duty until 8 am this morning."

"There was a lot going on last night," added the other policeman.

"A series of burglaries?" asked one of the workers.

"No," replied the policeman, "a charity event for ballet dancers with meniscus problems.

The Minister for State Funding for the Arts, the head of the State Coordination Office for Art Funding, the head of the State Funding Agency for Dance Art and the head of the State Funding Agency for Ballet Dance Art, as well as many other state employees and state-supported artists were there."

"I see," said the worker, "your colleagues had to ensure the safety of the people."

"No, I don't think there was a security problem," said the policeman. "Our colleagues had to regulate the traffic and pay attention to the parking regulations.

Last year there was a lot of confusion and the Minister for State Funding for the Arts had to wait five minutes for his parking space.

The head of the police considered this to be unacceptable. Therefore, this year he ordered all available police officers to regulate traffic and parking.

According to yesterday's orders, burglaries were only to be treated as a secondary matter and had no priority."

Relevance

The two policemen turned to leave.

"You have to come to the police station the day after tomorrow because we need a written confirmation of your report."

"Are you going to secure evidence here to follow up on this?" asked Laura.

"No," replied the policeman, "that doesn't pay off. Apart from a broken lock and a printer cover, nothing has been ruined or stolen."

"If I'd not prevented it, some machines would have been stolen and I would have been bankrupt due to the loss of production," said Laura.

The policeman shrugged his shoulders.

"There are too many ifs and buts," he replied. "After all, nothing really important has happened.

If machines will really be stolen and your company will indeed be bankrupted and ruined, we'll secure evidence. I can promise you that."

The two police officers said goodbye and left.

Support

Taio came with a new cover for the printer into Laura's factory workshop.

Since the part was not immediately necessary for the operation of the printer, he brought it in the evening.

"That was pretty dangerous what you did there," he said to Laura.

"Not really," replied Laura, "I'd have just run away if they had come towards me."

"You should have called me to help you."

"What would you have done?" asked Laura. "Would you have come with your kitchen knife to chase the burglars away and protect me?"

Taio thought for a moment, then smiled at her.

"I'd have held your hand to make you feel safe."

Laura laughed.

"You can do that without burglars being around."

Taio took her hand and she smiled at him.

They were looking into each other's eyes and slowly leaning towards each other and Minda entered the room full of verve.

"Wow, seems not to be the best time to enter," she said with a laugh. "You should hang a 'Do not disturb!' sign outside the door.

Do you have an idea where we're going for dinner? I'm ravenous."

Important Government Work

Laura was at the police station to make the required written record of her report.

She had reported to the reception and had been instructed to take a seat in the corridor.

After an hour she had asked how long it would take and had received the answer that it was impossible to predict.

Three hours had passed in the meantime, and she went to the reception desk again.

"Do you have any idea when my written report will be taken?" she asked the official.

"No, we're not just here for you."

"I must get back to my company. I have a job to finish today and will drop by on another day."

"That's not possible," replied the official, "today is your appointment. We have a lot to do, we can't wait for you."

Laura looked at him in astonishment. "I just waited three hours for you, what makes you think my work is less important than yours?"

"We're a state institution, of course our work is more important than yours. If you leave now, your report will be dropped altogether."

"I'm sorry," said Laura, "my customers are waiting for their merchandise."

She turned around and left the police station.

Not a Service Company

Did she really think she was in a hotel where we have to look after her needs, thought the reception desk officer. We are a state institution, not a service company.

We do what is right for the well-being of citizens, not what citizens want.

He wondered about the selfishness of people. They all wanted their concerns to be taken care of.

They should take an example from him. He had been sitting here at this counter for years, in order to serve the general public without complaining or thinking of himself.

I am a servant of the public, he thought proudly.

His supervisor called him.

"You must go on duty tomorrow too. A colleague is ill. You will get a bonus for the extra hours." He hung up.

How dare he, thought the official. I am not here to be taken advantage of by the others.

He decided to call in sick tomorrow as well.

There are even longer waiting times for applicants when two officials are ill, he thought, but that is not my problem.

I am not a servant of the public, he thought proudly.

State Interests

"The police officer told me over the phone that it wouldn't be possible to carry out individual investigations into every case of crime affecting individual citizens or individual companies because of the personnel costs involved."

Laura was talking to the lawyer.

"If it is possible for people working in state institutions to take taxpayers' money away from each citizen or company individually, it should also be possible to treat each case of crime individually."

"There are simply other interests," replied the lawyer. "In the case of the money taken from the taxpayers, it is about the means that politicians and civil servants themselves need for their own existence.

There is no direct benefit for civil servants and politicians in individual investigations of crimes affecting citizens.

The only interest that politicians have in this case is that the issue doesn't become important for too many citizens and could then influence their voting behaviour.

Your interests as an individual are not relevant to the people working in state institutions; you have to take care of them yourself."

"But the police, the military and the judiciary are the true tasks of the state," said Laura. "This is what we pay taxes for. For all other things, responsible citizens don't need state institutions. If the state didn't take care of the police, it would no longer have any reason to exist."

"If you want your own protection against burglary, you must hire a private security company to check your factory workshop at night at certain intervals," said the lawyer.

"Then it would be more reasonable if the police officially didn't take up the duty, and I'd pay less tax for them. I'd be able to use the money that the state then doesn't take away from me for a private security service," said Laura.

"That would definitely be an advantage for you. If the private security service doesn't fulfil its duties, you could sue it for damages. But you have no legal claim against the police for not fulfilling their duties.

But it would be a disadvantage for the state institutions, as they would lose tax revenue. In return, they wouldn't have any relief as they already don't provide the service," said the lawyer.

Leading Companies

"Oh, yes, there's still the matter of the blood pressure monitors."

The Minister for Economic Affairs and the head of the Employers' Association were sitting in an elegant restaurant drinking an aperitif with their dinner. The latter charged these dinners under the heading of public relations alternately to the Employers' Association and to the company where he was employed.

"Our sales in the non-medical sector have fallen sharply because of competition from some small company. Now the head office is on my case about it.

Politics should help us. We are a leading company after all."

"Of course," replied the Minister, "medical technology is an important economic sector with high growth potential. We need large leading companies in this field in order to give politicians the opportunity to intervene on the basis of planning studies.

We will set up a funding budget for leading companies in the medical technology sector and establish a steering committee, which will be jointly staffed by the state and the leading companies, in order to achieve a rapid allocation of taxpayers' money to the leading companies."

"It is particularly important to me," he added, "that we have shavings of truffles over the risotto. This gives a very exquisite taste."

State Support

Laura had met up again with her three friends for dinner on Saturday evening, this time at Jala's flat.

Jala told Laura that she had read in the newspaper that a large company that also produces blood pressure monitors had been appointed as a leading company and had received a lot of taxpayers' money as a grant.

She asked Laura what effect this would have on her business.

"I can't judge that yet," replied Laura. "I hope that the better quality of our blood pressure monitors will convince customers.

The fact is that up to now we've been able to offer our better quality at a lower price, as we've produced much more cost-effectively than the leading company.

This is now over, because the leading company can sell its poorer products cheaper because of taxpayers' money."

"But according to the newspaper, the leading company only receives taxpayers' money for research," said Jala, "but not to lower prices."

"This is just a cover-up," said Laura. "The money that they used to put into developing devices is now paid by the taxpayer, and they can now use it to make their products cheaper.

The procedure is ultimately only to the detriment of the customers.

My customers buy my blood pressure monitors because they give them more benefit than the devices of the leading company.

At the same time, I have to make every effort to meet the needs of the customers in the best possible way in order to sell my blood pressure monitors.

The leading company now receives taxpayers' money, whether or not it meets the needs of its customers.

In other words, customers no longer have such a great influence on how the equipment is built. Their needs and wishes become less important.

The demands of the customers become less important compared to the selfish motives of the politicians and civil servants who distribute the taxpayers' money to the leading company.

The grotesque thing is that the customers and I have to finance the damage that employees of the state institutions cause us, with our taxpayers' money.

We have to pay taxes so that politicians and officials can intervene in the market and allow companies to bypass customer needs."

Managed Economy and Market Economy

"What Laura says about her company applies to the entire market."

Minda looked at Jala.

"When politicians and civil servants tried to run the economy, the results were always bad and often even catastrophic."

"It is theoretically possible to plan the economy," interjected Efia, "so it should work in practice."

"Not even theoretically," replied Minda.

"No institution, whether governmental or non-governmental, is able to centrally collect and exploit all the local information that exists in the minds of customers and entrepreneurs.

This local information, which includes customer wishes and the new ideas of the entrepreneurs, is constantly changing and developing.

The lack of information leads to a permanent misuse of resources by the state-controlled economy. A permanent waste.

There are also major problems in the practical implementation of a state-controlled economy.

In such an economy, what the most influential organisations and groups currently want is done or, more precisely, what their leaders want is done. This is then dictated by the politicians.

The actual customer, be it an entrepreneur or the end user, is of secondary importance for a state-controlled economy; the use of resources is determined by these influential organisations and their leaders.

This leads to waste and misuse of resources, to the benefit of those organisations that influence politicians.

In a free market economy, it is the customer's wish that count. Through his needs, everyone is involved in deciding which goods or services the entrepreneurs will produce.

A free entrepreneur must always bring benefits to his customers, otherwise his business will perish, regardless of size.

Even very large corporations have gone bankrupt because they didn't comply with the wishes of their customers.

At the same time, priority is given to customer benefit, which means that there is no waste and that resources are used optimally. Those companies that do not use resources optimally will not be able to survive. Their products will become too expensive and customers will not buy them.

The customer decides, no one else does, and everyone can exert influence as a customer.

The free market economy – capitalism – is a system under the command and for the benefit of each individual. It is the only economic system in which all people are equal."

A Sad Example

"A sad example of what I've just been talking about is England," said Minda. "The country where the development of modern industry began in the eighteenth century and which was a leading industrial nation for 160 years.

In the 1920s, the economy there began to be increasingly state-controlled, and from the second half of the 1940s onward, state control was considerably tightened.

Twenty-five years later, the economy was hopelessly damaged.

Industry had reached a level comparable to that of countries that had not yet been able to develop an industry.

Groups of politicians and trade unions had asserted their individual group interests without regard to the needs of the customers. This brought the entire economic cycle to the brink of collapse.

Of course, these groups claimed to represent the general interest.

At the end of the 1970s, when it was clear to every responsible person that things could not go on like this, people began to leave this aberration behind.

But for many industries this came too late. They were irrevocably ruined by state intervention.

Now, after forty years, the situation has improved again, but it will never reach such heights again.

Thirty years of state control were enough to ruin the results of 160 years of free market economy in a lasting way.

This sad example should actually deter anyone who advocates state economic governance."

The Pretence of Knowledge

"Isn't it nevertheless good if politicians, advised by scientists, intervene to guide the economy and restrict entrepreneurs in their free decisions?" asked Jala. "Scientists commit themselves to rationality and are free of ideological delusions."

"Why should scientists be more faultless than other people and not be subject to ideological blindness?" asked Minda.

"Look at Paul Samuelson, for example," she said. "He won the Nobel Prize for Economics. He was and is a recognised scientist.

In 1989, he wrote the following in a recognised textbook, 'The Soviet economy is proof that, contrary to what many skeptics had earlier believed, a socialist command economy can function and even thrive.'

A few months later, the partner states of the Soviet Union collapsed for economic reasons and two years later, the Soviet Union collapsed itself.

It was clear to anyone interested in the subject at the time that there was a serious shortage of basic goods in the planned economy states. Even people who lived far away from these countries knew this.

My mother, who was a teenager at the time, said that any schoolchild who was interested in geography could get this information from the newspaper and just about everybody knew.

Nevertheless, a renowned scientist and Nobel Prize winner included these obviously false statements in his textbook without an outcry from his colleagues. He is still highly praised today.

Another Nobel Prize winner in economics, who is still alive, visited Venezuela in 2007 and commented very positively on the conditions there.

He said, 'Venezuela has taken advantage of high oil prices to implement policies that benefit its citizens and promote economic development.'

In a World Bank report of the same year titled 'Doing Business 2008', the following sentence was written about Venezuela, 'Venezuela had the largest negative reforms. Doing business there was already hard. In 2006/07 it got harder.'

In the Ease of Doing Business Index, Venezuela was ranked 172 out of the 178 countries surveyed.

A few years later, as a result of these difficulties for entrepreneurial activity, Venezuela was in economic chaos and the population was impoverished.

Nevertheless, a renowned scientist and winner of the Alfred Nobel Memorial Prize said these things without an outcry from his colleagues. He is still being praised today, and his prize has never been taken away from him."

"What makes scientists claim things that so obviously contradict the facts?" asked Laura.

"I don't think you can give a general answer to that," said Minda. "I think it often has personal reasons. These people are very intelligent, and they have learned a lot. They can't accept that the individual person lacks the many pieces of information that are distributed among all other individual people.

Individuals are therefore not in a position to manage the economy and society in a meaningful way from the top down. Friedrich August Hayek, also a Nobel Prize winner for economics, called the belief that everything can be controlled from the top down the pretence of knowledge.

But these people are not prepared to accept the impossibility of centrally controlling society through state planning or state redistribution.

It offends their pride. They do not want to admit that despite their intelligence, it is only a pretence of knowledge and that their theories of controlling the economy and society do not work.

Instead, they prefer to deny the facts in order to preserve their theories.

Just because someone is a scientist does not mean that he automatically behaves rationally."

Customer Benefits

The head of the Judo Association had received a prototype of a blood pressure monitor from Laura, with the agreed additional functions implemented. Laura thought that with its many additional functions, the designation as a blood pressure monitor was actually far too restrictive.

The athletes had tested the device and the head of the Judo Association had just called Laura to tell her about it.

"We're very impressed with the additional features the blood pressure monitor now has. Our original expectations have even been exceeded.

The athletes who tested the prototype are very satisfied. It worked perfectly and was very practical to use.

We're now definitely in business. As agreed, I'll come by the day after tomorrow so that we can put the order in writing."

"I'm delighted that we've succeeded in adapting the device so perfectly to your requirements," said Laura.

"Yes, we're also very satisfied, we were looking for a device with these functions.

By the way, I'll meet the head of the Athletics Association today. I'll tell him about your device because I think that this could also be interesting for these athletes."

"Thank you, that's very kind of you," said Laura. "If he has any questions, he can always call me."

"You're welcome. We're also always very happy to receive useful information from the Athletics Association, and your equipment is really very good."

They said goodbye and ended the conversation.

General Interest

"It is of great advertising value for us to supply the equipment for the Judo Association," said the head of the Employers' Association.

He was having dinner with the Minister for Economic Affairs and the Minister for Sport.

"Why didn't you get the contract?" asked the Minister for Sport.

"The Judo Association has special wishes regarding the design of the device, which the competing company has fulfilled," said the head of the Employers' Association. "I will eat the stuffed pheasant breast."

"Why don't you simply fulfil the wishes as well," asked the Minister for Sport. "Is there rosemary in the pheasant breast?"

"We don't have any technicians who can make such changes," replied the head of the Employers' Association.

"So far we have mainly delivered to state hospitals, and their special requests were not of interest to us as they had to buy from us in the general interest anyway, on the instructions of the Minister of Health.

But we have taken great care not to overlook the general interest.

The daughter of the Minister of Health was given a position in our company in the general interest. It was a position created especially for her.

She is now responsible for specialised, integrated communication on general interest issues and receives a very good salary.

We also have an additional trade union representative in the company, who is paid by us in the general interest.

The needs of the general public are very important to us. As a leading company we also have a social responsibility. Most of the time they have rosemary in the pheasant breast here."

"The leading companies are of great importance, also in social terms," said the Minister for Economic Affairs. "I will also eat the stuffed pheasant breast today."

"The general interest is also an important issue in sport," said the Minister for Sport. "I will point out to the head of the Judo Association that there are higher values than his selfish customer benefit and he has to buy the equipment from you. Basically, I would like to point out that rosemary goes very well with the pheasant breast stuffing."

General Interest and Selfishness

"The device of the leading company is of much less use to the athletes," said the head of the Judo Association.

He was speaking to the Minister for Sport, who had told him to buy the blood pressure monitors from the state-approved leading company and not from Laura.

"When you buy the blood pressure monitors, you must not only have the interests of the athletes in mind," replied the Minister for Sport.

"What other interests matter? The athletes are the customers who use these devices," said the head of the Judo Association.

"There are higher values than customer benefit, the general interest comes first."

"Why is it contrary to the general interest to buy a device that is best suited to our needs and provides the greatest benefit to us as customers?"

"I have already told you that it is in the general interest that you buy the device from the leading company. Leading companies are important for the state. Your petty customer benefit is secondary here."

"Who defines what is in the general interest anyway?"

"The political leadership of the state, of course, who knows what's in the general interest."

"What's the benefit to the general public if we have poor equipment, and thus poorer opportunities in our training and consequently poorer chances of success in competitions?"

"Your chances of success are not important for the general public after all. What is important is that the leading companies receive financial resources.

We can also imagine that you, as head of the Judo Association, will receive a salary from the state in the future. This would be in the general interest, provided you are prepared to act in the general interest and buy the blood pressure monitors from the leading company."

The leader of the Judo Association shook his head.

"We'll buy the equipment as planned, not from the leading company. The devices of the leading company are simply worse. The Judo Association is independent of the state, and we must use our money in such a way that it brings the greatest benefit to our athletes."

"If this is the case, I will be forced to cancel the state subsidies for your youth judo training.

As a state, we are committed to higher interests. Your petty selfishness is repulsive.

We will also withdraw funding for the World Cup."

"But it was your idea as Minister for Sport that we should apply for the World Cup. We would never have done it on our own because we cannot afford it. Besides, we've already put a lot of money into the preparation, which would then be lost."

"This is your problem. If you are so selfish as to act against the general interest and not to buy from the leading company, you must expect consequences," concluded the Minister for Sport.

Wait and See

"A problem has arisen."

Laura was sitting in her office. The head of the Judo Association had just called her.

"The Minister for Sport has threatened to cut funding for youth judo training if we don't buy the blood pressure monitors from the leading company.

If I have my way, we'll still buy the equipment from you. The many additional functions that you've developed for us simply result in an optimal device for our application."

"I'm glad to hear that," said Laura.

"But I can't decide that alone," said the head of the Judo Association. "This decision has to be voted on by the board of the Judo Association. There must be a majority for us to try to change the financing of the youth judo training. It won't be easy to find sufficient funds for this financing.

We'd have to cancel the World Cup then, even though we've already put some money into it.

Unfortunately, the purchase is therefore currently a completely open decision. I can't promise you anything."

"Thank you for informing me of this," replied Laura, "and I hope that our planned cooperation will nevertheless come about."

"I hope so, too," said the head of the Judo Association.

They said goodbye and ended the conversation.

The Planning Politician

At the same time as Laura's telephone call with the head of the Judo Association, the Minister for Economic Affairs was sitting in the back of his official car. His chauffeur was driving him home in the evening traffic. He had just returned from a dinner with the head of the state central bank.

He did not remember the conversation with him well, as he did not like him.

He considered him an arrogant busybody who was always talking about some economic theory to show how intelligent he seemed to be. The Minister for Economic Affairs thought these theories were just empty talk.

Inside the car it was quiet. One heard nothing of the traffic noise outside. The Minister for Economic Affairs thought of the remarks made by the head of the state central bank.

"Surely politicians can plan and steer the economy, even if he doesn't believe so," he muttered to himself.

Of course, he knew that those states where planned economies were implemented had collapsed economically.

He was also aware that in those states where attempts had been made to steer parts of the economy through politics in order to circumvent the rules of the free market, large sums of taxpayers' money had been wasted and the economic situation had deteriorated at the same time.

However, he did not attribute the countless failed cases to a fundamental problem. On the contrary, he thought that the reason was that the people who had implemented it were incapable.

In his view, the appropriate people would have been able to manage and plan a country's economy centrally.

He felt able to do so. He just sat up. He always did this when he felt particularly suited to a task and the urge to act flowed through him.

"That's what I'm doing successfully right now with my policy on leading companies," he muttered.

He proudly felt that his level-headed, planning overview led the country's economy in the right direction.

"Only small-minded people," he muttered, "can believe that economic planning by politicians doesn't work."

"A country's economy can be planned centrally, but it needs people of my intellectual stature to realise that," he muttered with certainty.

He reached into the pocket of his jacket and took out a packet of acid drops. When he tried to take one out, it was empty.

He railed against his assistant. She was responsible for getting the drops. She had observed his habits and decided to put a packet on his table every Monday.

"Completely absurd," he muttered, "as if my consumption of acid drops could be measured. Today is Thursday and I have none left.

What would she do if I didn't eat any acid drops at all because an entrepreneur had developed drops with a whole new flavour and I wanted to eat them instead?"

He shook his head at the views of his assistant. "Only bureaucrats who deny reality," he muttered, "can believe that a person's consumption of acid drops can be planned."

"People's consumption of acid drops cannot be planned, but it takes people of my intellectual stature to realise that," he muttered with certainty.

Then he fell asleep in the back seat of his official car.

The Planning Central Banker

The head of the state central bank looked at his reflection with satisfaction. He had just come home from dinner with the Minister for Economic Affairs and was standing in front of the mirror in his large cupboard. He thought about the evening while he was changing his clothes.

The conversation with the Minister for Economic Affairs during dinner had bored him. He despised the politicians and thought that they were uneducated babblers who had no idea about economics and money.

He laughed at the Economics Minister's idea regarding the leading companies. As if the economy of the whole state could be controlled so easily. This system with its millions of actors and the knowledge that was distributed in the minds of millions of people.

It was clear to him that he was the only one who could centrally control this system using the key interest rates of the central bank.

He was free to lower or raise interest rates as he wished and even expropriate people with negative interest rates on their savings accounts. No one could prevent this. The central bank was politically independent by law.

Of course, he knew from his comprehensive education that such interest rate manipulations as he had carried out in the past had always led to high currency devaluation or catastrophic stock market collapses.

But he also knew that his interest rate manipulations were different. He was much cleverer than his predecessors had been in the last 150 years and knew much more.

Even if his interest rate manipulations had so far not had the effect he expected, this did not affect him.

He knew that reality would have to follow his theory.

His theory was flawless and faultless. Reality could not escape it. Reality would have to follow his theory.

"It must, it must!" he cried euphorically.

He looked happily at his reflection and shouted out, "You are the smartest. You are the greatest. Reality will obey your theory. It must!"

Unplanned in the Moonlight

Laura had eaten dinner with Taio after her phone call with the head of the Judo Association.

Then they had gone into the park and sat down on a bench.

It was late and they were alone. It was a beautiful September evening. All around them the crickets were chirping, and the moon shone in a clear sky.

They both looked at the pond that lay calmly before them in the full moon light and let their minds wander.

"Since I started the second company," said Laura, "there have been so many unforeseen events in my private and professional life that I almost don't know what it was like before."

"Events often turn out differently than planned," replied Taio smiling.

Laura also smiled at him, and he put his hand on hers.

They were looking into each other's eyes and slowly leaning towards each other and the wood of the bench broke with a rotten crack.

They fell backwards into the grass.

"You're right," said Laura, as they looked at each other in shock.

Then they both started to laugh as the moon shone on their faces and the crickets chirped happily.

Prison Again

"Maybe I'll have to go to prison again," said Flora.

She was sitting with Laura in her sister's flat.

"Why's that?" asked Laura.

"An official of the Admissions Office claims I insulted him."

"What did you say to him?"

"I told him that he didn't know anything about the winter clothes business."

"Okay," said Laura, "tell the whole story."

"I bought a thousand pairs of woollen gloves last spring at a bargain price. When it got cold in the mornings six weeks ago, around the beginning of October, I thought now was the right time to sell. I then sold the gloves on the street within three days. Of course, this time I reported this to the tax office the day before and also to the Admissions Office, as you had told me.

Two weeks later a letter arrived from the Admissions Office. They wrote that you cannot register in writing but must appear in person.

I then called and said that the whole thing was already done and that they didn't need to pursue this any further.

The official then said that I'd broken the law by selling the gloves without reporting the activity to the Admissions Office. I replied that I'd made the report and hadn't had time to come in person.

He said that I should have appeared in person first; later, once the authorisation had been granted, I could have sold the gloves.

I said to him that he didn't know much about the winter clothing business. I sold all the gloves on the street in those days because it was getting surprisingly cold. A few days later people would have had time to buy the gloves in shops, and I wouldn't have been able to sell my gloves."

"You don't have to go to prison for that?" asked Laura.

"I have received a fine from the Admissions Office for illegal business activity that is higher than the turnover I made with the gloves.

And yesterday I received a summons from the court to a trial for insulting a public official."

Laura shook her head.

"It's time for you to talk to the lawyer."

Night Watchman State

"You won't have to go to prison, maybe a conditional prison sentence, but another heavy fine awaits you in any case."

Laura and Flora were sitting in the lawyer's office. They had told her about the proceedings of the Admissions Office against Flora.

"What about the fine to be paid to the Admissions Office for the alleged illegal business activity?" asked Flora.

"We can reduce it by a third at most, with the official reduction being two thirds. However, one third will go to the person who approves the reduction."

"Can't we even do that without this disgusting corruption?" asked Laura.

"Yes, in principle, but we already talked about this when you founded your company.

The outcome of an appeal is extremely uncertain and even if you're successful, you've lost so much money due to the costs of the proceedings that success is pointless, and it would have been cheaper for you to pay the whole penalty right away."

"Can't you get away without a court case by making such a payment to a judicial official?" asked Flora.

"No, this can only be done if you deal with an administrative authority. You're far too insignificant for the judiciary to get involved. You would have to know a lot more people in the state apparatus and offer a lot more money."

"What's happening here is completely absurd," said Laura thoughtfully. "Flora comes into conflict with the state apparatus just because she sells gloves without harming others. She has properly paid the taxes on the business. The state took them without resistance, even though the activity was allegedly illegal.

Then she's accused of insulting an official just because an official feels that way. The entire state apparatus has a life of its own here, one which offers no benefit to the citizens."

"You mustn't forget that many citizens are themselves active in the state apparatus," replied the lawyer. "Also, many politicians have only been active in the state apparatus. These people have their livelihoods in the state apparatus and are interested in it expanding its activities."

"But the citizens maintain a state apparatus for the purpose of taking over certain service functions which facilitate coexistence, not for patronising them and giving special status to civil servants."

"Yes," said the lawyer, "but as soon as you give someone the power to order something, he will gradually expand that power. That's in the nature of human beings. To prevent this increasing paternalism and such senseless incidents as in Flora's case, one would have to regulate state institutions strictly to those areas that one really wants to solve collectively."

"A night-watchman state," said Laura. "I had a conversation about this some time ago. State institutions which, like a medieval night watchman, are paid by the citizens to provide security but have no power over the living conditions of the citizens and cannot tell them how to live their lives ..."

"... and just like a night watchman, they can't dictate whether you can sell gloves or not," added Flora.

"Yes," said Laura, "military, police and judiciary, a politically mature citizen doesn't need more state institutions."

Morals and Joy

"Isn't it very unsatisfactory for you that you always have to deal with such cases of abuse of power and corruption in your profession?" Laura asked the lawyer.

"I firmly believe," she replied, "that a functioning judicial system is the prerequisite for individual freedom and prosperity.

Of course, such a system can also be misused. A dictatorship can also build on a functioning judicial system.

In a legal system that's carried out by human beings, mistakes and abuses occur time and again, as you yourself must constantly experience.

Nevertheless, I don't want to be put off by that. I like my job and I consider it right and important.

I work to keep the judicial system functioning and I'm part of it. I help people to cope with the legal system.

This is something that corresponds to my moral concepts based on an ethic of the rule of law and individual freedom.

It is a beautiful profession. Even though I keep coming across cases where the system is abused.

I also like it when I'm successful at work and I earn well, which I enjoy a lot because it gives me independence."

Strong State

Jala, Minda and Laura were sitting in Efia's flat. It was Saturday afternoon. They had helped Efia put up a new wardrobe and now they were talking.

Laura told them about the conversation she and Flora had had with the lawyer.

"Don't you think," asked Efia, "that you need a strong state, which has many more rights than a night watchman state, for other things? For example, when an epidemic breaks out and protective measures need to be taken?"

"A strong state with many rights isn't required for this," replied Minda.

"The opposite is true," she added. "Think about where the last major epidemic broke out. That was in a strong state where citizens had few rights.

There, politicians kept the outbreak of the epidemic quiet for a long time so as not to jeopardise their power. Doctors who pointed this out were threatened by the police. There was no free media there.

In a night watchman state, such a thing would never have happened. Nobody would have been able to threaten the doctors, and the free media would have reported quickly about the new disease. Everything would have been transparent.

In a night watchman state, an epidemic of this magnitude would never have occurred. All citizens would have been informed by the media from the outset and doctors would have quickly taken rational measures to treat sick people before the whole thing escalated into an epidemic.

Of course, in the event of an epidemic, quarantine measures can lead to a short-term restriction of personal rights, but these measures do not require a strong state.

If quarantine measures become necessary in a night watchman state, they are supported by the majority of the population because they are transparently and rationally explained and imposed by a democratically elected government.

Of course, not everyone complies with the law, but a night watchman state has sufficient institutions in the form of police and judiciary to control the quarantine laws.

There is no plausible reason why doctors and nurses should be civil servants.

In order to prevent and combat epidemics, you do not need a strong state. You need a transparent, rational state that is accepted by a free, self-determined population."

Responsibility

"I see you've placed the sign saying 'Exit' as I told you to. Even in the size I prescribed."

The official from the State Industrial Inspectorate was standing again in Laura's factory workshop and pointed to the workshop door.

"A big sign," said Laura. "It was expensive."

"Yes," said the official, "there is nothing you can do about it. That's what is prescribed in Section 231 of the Industrial Workshops Act."

"My lawyer, who saw the sign yesterday, said that I wouldn't need the sign at all under Section 232 of the Industrial Workshops Act."

"Really?" asked the officer. "I will take a look at that."

He placed the thick folder, which he had pressed to his body with one arm, on a table in front of them. He was leafing through it and reading in silence.

"That's really quite funny," he said. "Your lawyer is right. You didn't have to buy the sign at all.

Nothing this funny has happened to me in a long time." He shook his head and laughed. "I was wrong.

You've spent money on something you don't need. Well, these things happen in life.

Unfortunately, I have to leave now. Otherwise, I won't be able to get to the office before closing time and you would have to pay expensive extra hours for my visit. Good afternoon."

He left the workshop still laughing.

Independence and Values

"Our agreement remains."

The head of the Judo Association was speaking to Laura in her office.

"We've decided not to be blackmailed by the Minister for Sport and to finance ourselves in future only through advertising contracts from private companies. All the club leaders present were in agreement.

We are athletes and our success is based on our performance. That's why we agreed that we want to follow this principle in our business relations as well. You get the order because you deliver the best product. Your blood pressure monitor converted for our purposes offers the greatest benefit to us.

We don't want to get involved in the strange machinations of the Minister for Sport to buy a product from a so-called leading company that's more expensive and doesn't meet our expectations.

Even if the financial damage we'd suffer could be compensated for by state subsidies from taxpayers' money, the product would still not meet our expectations."

"The public authorities have other objectives," said Laura.

"You're right," said the head of the Judo Association. "The minister's aim was only to justify the activity of the State Agency for the Promotion of Sport and to force us to buy the blood pressure monitors of the leading company."

"Do you no longer receive any state support for youth judo training at all?" asked Laura. "The official aim of the support has always been to get young people into Judo so that they get more exercise."

"No, the subsidies for the youth have now been cancelled because we bought your blood pressure monitors and not those of the leading company.

But we're happy about it. The success of our judo athletes is based on their own performance and not on the exploitation of the achievement of others against their will.

That's why our association should be based on its own performance and not on a non-transparent allocation of taxpayers' money generated by the taxpayers' performance.

The bureaucratic apparatus of the State Agency for the Promotion of Sport, which distributes taxpayers' money without any personal contribution, contradicts the values of our athletes and thus also those of the association. We don't want to have anything to do with it anymore and want to be independent."

Independence and Cooperation

The leader of the Judo Association stood up, and they said goodbye.

"I look forward to our future cooperation," he said as he walked to the door.

"I find our cooperation ideal," he added. "You deliver a product that meets our needs, and we've no obligation to you. If the product meets our wishes, we'll buy it. If not, we won't.

At the same time, you sell us your product and fulfil our needs because you benefit from it. If you couldn't benefit from it, you wouldn't do so.

In this way, both sides have an advantage, completely voluntarily, without threatening or putting pressure on each other, as the Minister for Sport did with the Judo Association.

We're both independent and self-determined, and yet we cooperate to our respective advantage."

"Yes," said Laura, "I talked to a friend about it some time ago. That's the essence of the free market economy. It is voluntary cooperation from which everyone benefits."

"This is completely different from our cooperation with the State Ministry of Sport," said the head of the Judo Association.

"They put pressure on our Judo Association, withdraw state subsidies and threaten to found a state Judo Association just so we buy a product that doesn't meet our needs at all."

"It is somehow grotesque," he added, "that it is precisely the employees of state institutions, politicians and civil servants, who always emphasise the general interest and cooperation between people, who permanently try to prevent this voluntary cooperation in order to enforce their own group interests at the expense of others."

"Based on the experience I've had since the establishment of this company," replied Laura, "I think that this seemingly contradictory behaviour is a characteristic of people who run state institutions."

"Well," said the head of the Judo Association with a laugh, "fortunately, I won't have to deal with this apparatus so much in the future and better not waste any time thinking about the absurdities."

He shook Laura's hand and left.

Waste

On the way to the courthouse, where she wanted to attend Flora's trial, Laura thought about a technical detail that could optimise the production of her blood pressure monitor.

The optimisation would make it possible to produce the device with less energy consumption.

This would make it possible, Laura thought, to offer the device to customers at a lower price. At the same time, my company would reduce its indirect CO_2 emissions and thus help in the fight against climate change.

A horn signal near her shocked her out of her thoughts, and she thought again about the reason for her walk.

What a senseless waste of resources is caused by the state patronising people, she thought.

Instead of being able to think about improvements to my company that would save customers money and at the same time produce less greenhouse gas, I have to think about an absurd court case.

Instead of letting Flora work and act economically, which ultimately increases the prosperity of all, she must waste her time in permit procedures, court hearings and prison.

Instead of using her services to promote prosperity by negotiating contracts between companies, the lawyer must defend Flora against the accusations of the civil service.

Instead of the many employees of the civil service apparatus in the administration and the judiciary pursuing wealth promotion, they're busy preventing people from acting independently and imposing on them rules developed by an additional civil service and political apparatus.

This whole paternalism and restriction of people is a gigantic waste of resources, Laura thought.

These state restrictions are as if I tied my own feet together now and could only slowly and with difficulty hop on the way to court instead of walking briskly.

It is such a huge, senseless waste of human abilities.

Independent Judiciary

The trial was over. Afterwards, Laura and the lawyer were walking together back to their workplaces. Flora had already taken leave of them.

Laura looked at the lawyer. "The judge shouted at my sister and called her a stupid woman, without any consequences for herself.

At the same time, my sister will be detained for three days. She was sentenced to six months conditional detention and a heavy fine for telling the judge that she had no idea about the winter clothing business.

The judge has to obey the same laws as my sister, hasn't she?"

"Of course, judges must abide by the law," replied the lawyer.

"What are the consequences for the judge who shouted at and insulted my sister?"

"There are none. Certainly, her behaviour isn't right. You could also call it illegal, but that's a matter of interpretation. Those who might object are judges themselves and naturally allow themselves and their colleagues a great deal of freedom.

Yelling at the accused or making cynical remarks to them are considered normal behaviour that isn't in conflict with any law.

The judge who shouted at and insulted your sister is even considered a capable judge within the judiciary."

"Who supervises the judges?" asked Laura.

"An independent judiciary is the basis of our rule of law and the prerequisite for us to be able to live in a free society," said the lawyer.

"The supervision of the judges can therefore only be carried out by judges; anything else would be an outside influence and would open the door to arbitrariness."

"Does that work when a group supervises itself or doesn't this just lead to arbitrariness again?" asked Laura. "The judges are only human beings, with all their good and bad sides."

"It requires a high degree of moral integrity," replied the lawyer. "Of course, it is in human nature that not all judges have this."

"But the purpose of an independent judiciary is to prevent the abuse of power and arbitrary rule, not to establish the judiciary itself as an unassailable arbitrary system," said Laura.

"If you give people power over other people, there will always be those who abuse it. That's in the nature of human beings and unfortunately cannot be avoided," replied the lawyer.

Laura pondered. "Ultimately, the solution to this problem of abuse can only be that there are fewer laws that restrict people. Then there is less power that can be abused.

If my sister had been allowed to sell the gloves without any state restrictions, the judge would never have been able to shout at her, that she's a stupid woman. She couldn't have sentenced her to six months conditional imprisonment for insulting a judge."

"You're undoubtedly right. The most effective way to prevent the state abuse of power is not to allow any accumulation of state power."

Emotional Law

"The law is paramount in the courtroom. You must remember that," said the judge.

The young judge nodded eagerly.

The judge had returned to her office after Flora's trial. She was standing in front of a mirror and twitching at her hair. The young judge, who had been an associate judge at the trial, was standing a little way behind her.

"For us, only the words of the legal text apply, and we must stick to them. It isn't our private feelings that count, but the law."

The young judge nodded eagerly.

"Our personal opinion or attitude has no place in the enforcement of the law. We act rationally on the basis of the law."

The young judge nodded eagerly.

"Half a year," he noted, "to which this person has just been sentenced, which paragraph justifies the amount? To my shame, I must confess I can't find one."

"That stupid, insolent person. How does she think she can talk to me? Have you seen her hair? She probably has nothing else to do all day but groom her hair," the judge snorted excitedly and continued to twitch her hair angrily.

She turned energetically away from the mirror and turned towards the young judge.

"You'll find a paragraph that you can apply accordingly.

I've been a judge for thirty years now and I know that this woman deserves punishment. This is what my personal feeling tells me, based on my experience as a judge.

This is my personal opinion, and it is more important for a good judge than the text of the law."

The young judge nodded eagerly.

"A good judge acts on the basis of his emotions, which are based on his experiences."

The young judge nodded eagerly.

"In the courtroom, the personality of the judge is above the law. You must remember that!"

The young judge nodded eagerly.

New Paths

"I'll go abroad for at least three years," said Flora.

Flora, Laura, Taio and the lawyer stood together in front of the small steel door in the prison wall from which Flora had just come after serving three days in prison.

Flora looked happily at the others.

"Then my probationary period will be over, and I will no longer run the risk of having to serve six months in prison for some trivial thing.

Moreover, with the conditional prison sentence I'm not allowed to set up a business in this country anyway."

"A malicious action by the judge," said Laura. "She has made it impossible for you to start a business for three years."

"Do you know where you're going yet?"

"I'd like to try Georgia."

"Not a rich country," replied the lawyer. "The state economic governance has done much damage there in the twentieth century."

"But today the country offers many opportunities," said Flora.

"In the World Bank's Ease of Doing Business Ranking, it is among the top countries. Corruption has been pushed back very far and is steadily decreasing.

I've also heard that the people there are very hospitable.

I think it is a good place to implement my business plans without being harassed by state institutions or running the risk of having to serve my conditional sentence."

"That sounds good," said Laura, "although I'd rather have you near me."

Flora laughed. "We'll stay connected using video chat.

Besides, you've found someone special to be close to." She winked at Taio.

Laura and Taio took each other by the hand and laughed at each other.

"Now let's go to the same restaurant around the corner as after my last time in prison," said Flora. "I've fond memories of that, although hopefully today will be our last visit."

Freedom

"If you are as freedom-loving as Flora, you always get into trouble with the state authorities," said Taio.

After the four of them had eaten, Flora had said goodbye. The other three were driving to the lawyer's office in Taio's car to let her get off.

"She's constantly moving in a cage that restricts her freedom," replied the lawyer.

"I don't believe that freedom is something that you can or should let others assign to you," said Laura.

"Freedom is something you take.

Look at Flora. She doesn't worry about why these obstacles are present in her life. She just happily sets about overcoming the obstacles.

One is free when one is aware that one's own life is not subordinated to other people or institutions.

Similarly, the freedom of others means that their lives are not subordinated to you.

Even in a violent slave state it would never be possible to be pressed into total bondage with this awareness, even if one's own path in life is largely denied.

One cannot expect this awareness to be given or allowed. One must take freedom consciously for oneself.

This doesn't mean that there are no obstacles to overcome. There is always effort involved in living, that's nothing unusual. It is nothing to fear.

If you want to eat a piece of bread that you hold in your hand, you have to raise your hand to your mouth. If you want to look at the moon, you have to raise your head.

If one wants to be free, one must defend oneself against those who want to rule over others and against those who celebrate their own lack of freedom.

But that's nothing unusual. It is nothing to fear as a human being.

Freedom is not a gift that can be given or bestowed by anyone. Freedom doesn't fall to the individual by chance either.

Freedom is a state that one chooses on the basis of a rational decision without having to rely on others to accept that choice.

Freedom means to live one's life as one sees fit on the basis of one's own rational decisions without requiring or expecting the consent of others."

Further Ahead

Taio came to Laura's factory workshop to pick her up.

Laura yawned. "We have already completed the first part of the order of the Judo Association.

They've received enough advertising orders to finance it, even though the staff of the Minister for Sport are in the background trying to create a mood against the Judo Association."

She thought for a moment and said, "When I deal with state institutions, I often feel as if I'm taking part in a race where the spectators are constantly throwing rods between my legs."

She shook herself. "But no matter, we'll continue to meet on the free market. There customers will decide according to criteria that are important to them and not civil servants and politicians.

I have no need to fear this type of competition where performance and facts count."

Taio held out his hands to her. He smiled and said, "I can think of nothing that would make me happier than to join you in a race where the spectators are constantly throwing rods between our legs."

Laura laughed and put her hands in his.

Then they fell silent. They were looking into each other's eyes and slowly leaning towards each other and kissed.